A Hero for Leanda

A Hero for Leanda

by Andrew Garve

"A most agreeable and readable yarn. The only fault I found with it was that I became far too envious of the participants."
—*John W. Vandercook*

"Mr. Andrew Garve specializes in the pleasantly smooth, relatively non-violent type of English crime story. *A Hero for Leanda* preserves the tone while widening the theme."
—*The Times* [London] *Literary Supplement*

"An odd, fresh, pleasing tale.... The plot is simple but astutely twisted."
—Anthony Boucher,
The New York Times Book Review

"One can trust Mr. Garve to put a fresh twist to any situation, and the ending is a really lovely surprise."
—*Manchester Guardian*

"Told in Garve's seemingly effortless and unhurried style, this makes an absolutely first-rate suspense yarn, and its superb denouement completely fooled and delighted this reviewer."
—*San Francisco Chronicle*

Other titles by Andrew Garve available in Perennial Library:

A Hero for Leanda

by Andrew Garve

PERENNIAL LIBRARY
Harper & Row, Publishers
New York, Hagerstown, San Francisco, London

First PERENNIAL LIBRARY edition published 1978

ISBN: 0-06-080429-7

78 79 80 81 82 10 9 8 7 6 5 4 3 2

1

As soon as Mike Conway heard that his yacht *Tara* had been found he hurried down to the steel-pile jetty that was all Accra offered in the way of port facilities and, too worried to bargain, hired a surf boat at the coxswain's price to take him out to the reef. The young fisherman who had come upon the wreck that morning went with them as guide. The wind was now no more than a gentle breeze from the sea, but once outside the breakwater the African crew had to strain at their paddles to keep the boat head-on to the surf that never ceased to roll on the Ghana coast. Soon their strong black bodies, naked except for loincloths, were glistening with sweat in the warm, moist air. They grunted as they paddled, but that was the only sound they made. From a dozen other surf boats, plying between the jetty and the big cargo ships unloading at anchor, came a steady monotonous chant. But Conway's crew were silent, as though out of respect for his trouble.

In twenty minutes they had reached the coral. The surf boat

1

had stopped pitching now; there was only a slight swell in the lee of the reef and the surface of the water was scarcely ruffled. The fisherman began to call out directions; the coxswain, steering the boat with a long oar, maneuvered cautiously through the maze of coral heads. Conway gazed tensely over the high prow as a telltale patch of flotsam came into view—a floorboard, an empty paraffin can, a sodden chart, a fragment of the flag of Eire on a splintered pole. Suddenly the fisherman cried, "Look, massa, dey she is!" and pointed.

Conway stared down through the blue, transparent water. As he took in the scene, an involuntary groan escaped him. Until this moment he had never quite lost hope, even when the fisherman had described the wreck to him. He had buoyed himself up with the thought that a salvage operation might be possible, that the yacht might be raised and repaired. . . . Now he could see that *Tara* would never sail again. She had pounded herself to bits on the jagged coral and was lying broken-backed on the white sand three fathoms down, her bows stove in and her timbers crushed.

He stood in grim-faced silence, scarcely able to believe the extent of his ill fortune. He still didn't know exactly how the disaster had happened. Probably he never would. All he knew was that it had been none of his own making. He had gone ashore for an hour or two after dark, leaving *Tara* securely tied to one of the mooring rings on the jetty. Someone could have untied the rope to release another boat, and forgotten to make it fast again. Or someone might have loosed the yacht out of mischief, not foreseeing the devilish freak wind from the shore that would drive her out past the breakwater and onto the reef. If so, the

2

prank had cost Conway literally everything he possessed in the world except the shorts and shirt he was wearing, and his passport, and the few pounds in his pocket. The irony of it was almost unbearable. Singlehanded, he had sailed *Tara* over ten thousand miles of ocean, riding out a score of gales and surviving every kind of hazard. Disaster could have come at any time, but it had passed him by. Till now—in what should have been a safe harbor.

He turned away, unable to bear the sight any longer. *Tara* had been more to him than a fine ship. For years she had been his only home; for weeks at a time, his sole companion. He would miss her like hell.

"All right," he called to the coxswain roughly, "let's go."

Ashore, he wasted no time in vain regrets. He was a practical man, and there were urgent things to be done. With a bit of luck, he might still salvage some of his belongings before *Tara* finally broke up. There was an unexpired letter of credit for fifty pounds down in the cabin which, if still decipherable, should pay for the hire of an Aqua-Lung diver and leave something over. There were his references and diplomas, which he'd need if he was to get a decent job quickly. His treasured books would hardly be worth bringing up, but there were his clothes, his compass and sextant, his tools, his spare sails—all worth a bit. A couple of good divers might even be able to raise *Tara's* light engine. If so, he could overhaul it himself, and it would certainly fetch a few pounds.

With sweat pouring off him in the greenhouse heat of the afternoon, he made his way to the harbormaster's office to seek advice. As a yacht owner, a man of prestige and independence, he had had good and friendly service from the harbormaster. Now that he was hardly more than a survivor, things might be different. But the graying Negro was sympathetic and helpful. There was a contractor in the town, he said, who might undertake the salvage job, especially if Conway mentioned the letter of credit as proof that he could pay. Conway thanked him, and took the address, and plodded on. But the contractor was away up the coast on a job, and wouldn't be back till next day. Conway made an appointment, praying that the weather would hold.

The next thing was to start looking for work. He would soon be penniless, and he could think of few worse places to be penniless in than Accra. There were people he'd met in the town who might help him. That was one way. Influential-seeming men he'd been introduced to at the Yacht Club, at the European Club, when for a day or two he'd been something of a celebrity, a prized guest with a good story to tell. Cocoa planters, mining engineers, shipping men, who had entertained him lavishly—and several of whom he'd entertained himself, aboard *Tara*, and got on well with. They'd been decent people; they'd probably do their best to give him a leg up. The trouble was, he didn't want to ask them. He didn't want to feel obliged to anyone. Better, he thought, to keep the thing impersonal—to go along to the Labour Exchange and line up with the black men and offer what he had and take what there was. Ghana, he'd read, was in need of skilled men, and his qualifications were high. They were building a new harbor for ocean-going ships at Tema, just along the coast—there might be a suitable billet for him there. Of course,

4

he'd need a work permit. He'd have to see the immigration people again—and this time they wouldn't be coming out in a launch to meet him! He was land-bound, now, and could expect no special treatment. Soon, no doubt, he'd be red-tape-bound, too. He'd managed to get away from all that in *Tara*, but he'd have to face it now. He'd have to deal with self-satisfied bureaucrats, office boys who'd graduated to brief cases and couldn't forget it. There'd be lengthy interviews—perhaps humiliating ones. In this newly sovereign country there were plenty of officials who would enjoy humiliating a white man. Still, the sooner he started, the sooner he'd finish. He'd better get along to the Labour Exchange right away. . . . But when he looked at his watch he saw that it was five o'clock. All the offices would be closing. First thing tomorrow, then.

Meanwhile, he had to get through the evening. He could go back to the Rest House, where for a few shillings a night he'd been staying since *Tara's* disappearance—but there'd be nothing to do there except sit on the veranda and receive the unwanted condolences of his fellow guests. Better to keep moving, to walk on through the town—though he didn't much like the town, either. He'd never intended to stay in Accra for long—he'd called in for fresh food and supplies on his leisurely way round the Guinea coast, that was all. It was a squalid place, like most of these tropical ports. A façade of dignity and wealth, the British colonial front, and behind it a slum interior. Picturesque, of course, in a way—he remembered how intrigued he'd been by it when he'd first come ashore, full of his usual zest for new places and knowing that *Tara* was lying waiting for him in the harbor, a way of escape when he needed it. He'd strolled with

5

curiosity and pleasure among the stalls in the native quarter, among the tin buckets and old tires and alarm clocks, the silks and ivory and brass, and thought the scene as colorful and lively as an Eastern bazaar. Now he saw it all with a prisoner's jaundiced eye—the narrow, congested streets, the dark bodies jostling, the bare feet stirring the black dust, the blaring cars, the sightless beggars, the stench and the heat. He told himself that he'd have to get used to it, since he couldn't even raise the fare to leave it—that he soon would get used to it, think nothing of it, as other Europeans had. At thirty-two, he should have resilience enough for that. It wouldn't be the first port he'd had to stay and work in for a while—he'd been doing it, at intervals, for years, when supplies ran low and he needed money for the next leg of his travels. All the same, he wished he could have been shipwrecked in some more salubrious and temperate place, if he'd had to be shipwrecked at all.

He drifted around for an hour or so, postponing the first drink as long as he could because the later he left it the less the night would cost him. Then, about seven, he turned into a bar called the Come to Heaven. It had a cement floor with strips of worn coconut matting over it, and wicker chairs round beer-stained tables, and fairy lights over the bar counter, and sections of green-painted plywood to screen it from the rowdy street. The whitewashed walls were decorated with pin-up girls torn from Western magazines. It was a tawdry place, but it suited his pocket. He ordered a double Scotch at the bar and took it to a table near the entrance, where there was air of a kind. The place was about half full. There were four young Negroes in a corner,

6

drinking iced beer and arguing fiercely about politics. There was a very old man reading a newspaper, and two other men trying to arrange a deal of some sort, and a few laughing couples in gay shirts and tight cotton frocks. Conway was the only European, but no one took much notice of him. He drank his whisky slowly, making it last. Perhaps after all, he thought, he should have called on the Irish consul and tried to borrow a few pounds, sinking his pride. Anesthesia cost money, even in Heaven—he wouldn't get far on one double. He thought of the almost full bottle of Jameson that was lying in *Tara's* cabin, three fathoms down, and made a mental note to tell the Aqua-Lung chap about it. He'd barely touched it in weeks at sea, he'd never felt the need of it, but he could have done with it now—he could have sozzled it quietly on his own, instead of sitting in this lousy bar. A blast of syncopated music from a gramophone almost deafened him. He moved away from it, over to the other side of the doorway, but it didn't make much difference. You couldn't hope to get away from gramophones in Accra, anyway. As he settled down again, a blood-lusting mosquito stabbed at his ankle. Outside the entrance, a couple of children groveled in the gutter and a mangy dog nosed for scraps.

He finished his drink and counted his money. He could manage only one more double, if he was to pay his way at the Rest House. He was about to get up and go to the bar when another European came in—a little, elderly man, very dapper and prosperous-looking in a cream tussore suit and a cream Panama hat. He wore pince-nez and carried an ivory-topped cane. Conway had a feeling he'd seen the man somewhere before—perhaps at

7

the European Club. The Come to Heaven was surely off his beat?

The newcomer glanced around. His eyes met Conway's. He turned and ordered a glass of brandy, and then came toward Conway's table. He had short legs and small feet and his gait was mincing. At the table he raised his hat and gave a courtly little bow. What with the hat and the stick and the brandy, he seemed like a very polite juggler.

"Please forgive my intrusion," he said, "but are you not Mr. Michael Conway, the yachtsman?" His English was precise, but he had a slight accent which Conway couldn't place.

"I *was!*" Conway said ruefully.

"Ah, yes . . . I heard this afternoon that the remains of your boat had been found. A total loss, they say. That is very bad luck."

Conway nodded.

"May I introduce myself? My name is Venizelos. I manage the General and West Coast Trading Company here. . . ." The little man put his glass down on the table. "Would you, perhaps, allow me to buy you a drink, Mr. Conway?"

"I would indeed," Conway said, "if you'll forgive me for not returning the compliment. I'm as near broke as makes no odds."

"I understand. . . . Let me see, Scotch whisky, is it?"

"It is."

The drink, when it came, was huge. Conway lifted the glass gratefully. "Your very good health, sir!"

"And better fortune to you in the future!" Venizelos said. He produced a case of cheroots, offered one to Conway, who declined, and put them away again. "It was, of course, an accident in a thousand. But so final. As soon as I read that your boat had

8

gone from the harbor in the storm, I feared she must have ended up on the reef."

"It always seemed likely," Conway said.

"She was not, I suppose, insured?"

Conway shook his head. "There's no insurance for single-handed ocean yachtsmen—not at a premium I could ever afford to pay. If you travel that way, you have to take the knocks yourself."

"You seem to be taking this knock with great fortitude, Mr. Conway. May I say that I admire you? I have read, with the greatest interest, all that has been written about you in the newspapers here. I do not pretend to understand what takes a young man alone across the seas, for such long periods, but to travel like that, and to arrive, is a great achievement. You obviously have both skill and courage. . . . And what, if I may ask, do you intend to do now?"

"Get a job here as soon as I can," Conway said.

"Have you anything particular in mind?"

"I was trained as an engineer before I took to the sea. I imagine I'll find something in my own line before long."

Venizelos nodded slowly. "There are openings here, I am sure —but only the top jobs are paid well, the contract jobs, and they are rarely allotted to applicants on the spot. . . . Then again, I wonder how you would like it, settling down here? The Coast is not everyone's choice for a home."

"It wouldn't be mine in a million years," Conway said, "but beggars can't be choosers. Anyway, I don't intend to settle down. I shall work till I've saved enough money to buy another boat, and then I'll be off again."

"And how long do you think that will take?"

Conway gave a wry smile. "Quite a while, I should think—but what else can I do?"

"Ah!" Venizelos leaned forward a little. "Now that is what I would like to talk to you about. . . . I have a confession to make, Mr. Conway. It was not by accident that we met here this evening. I have been—keeping an eye on you. To be precise, I followed you here."

Conway looked at him in astonishment. "What on earth for?"

"Because I have a proposition to put before you."

"Really . . . ? Well, I'll be happy to listen—though if it's anything to do with your trading company I doubt if it'll be up my street."

"It has nothing to do with my trading company."

"What's on your mind, then?"

"Unfortunately," Venizelos said, "I cannot give you any details. I am only an agent in this matter—you would have to see my principal. And as there is some urgency, you would have to see him without delay. He is at Biarritz, in France. You would have to go there."

Conway stared at him. "Are you serious?"

"I have never been more serious."

"It's a long way to go for an interview, isn't it?"

"Not if you fly. Naturally all your expenses would be paid."

"But—who *is* your principal? What does he do?"

"I am afraid I cannot tell you that, either," Venizelos said. "But if you agree to go and see him, you will be given all necessary instructions. Your travel and hotel expenses will be taken care of. In addition, you will receive a cash payment of five hundred pounds, irrespective of the outcome of the interview. If, when you have heard what my principal has to say, you feel you must decline his proposition, you will be flown back here at his expense—or, if you prefer it, to some other place. If you agree to his proposition, you will receive more money—a very great deal more. . . . Well, Mr. Conway, are you interested?"

"I'm fascinated," Conway said. The crow's-feet that fanned from the corners of his eyes deepened as his weather-beaten face creased in a slow grin. "You know, Mr. Venizelos, when I was in Cape Town a few months ago I saw a movie that I'm now reminded of. An American, I think it was, was approached by a stranger in a tropical port, very much like this one, with a proposition. In the movie, though, the stranger said, 'I must warn you that the work might be dangerous.' "

Venizelos nodded. "*Your* work might have its dangers, too."

"I thought perhaps it might! Now in this movie I'm telling you about, the American said, 'I guess I can take care of myself,' or words to that effect. That was all right for him, he was a movie star. I'm not. I'd want to know a great deal about the dangers, and they'd probably put me off right away. . . . This American also said, 'But I draw the line at murder and dope-running'— and I'm with him there. I draw quite a lot of lines myself."

"You need have no anxiety on that score," Venizelos said. "What my principal would have to suggest would be quite— ethical."

"One man's ethics could be another man's crime," Conway said.

Venizelos gave a delicate little shrug. "You can always turn the proposition down, Mr. Conway. There will be absolutely no obligation—and whatever happens, you will be the richer by five hundred pounds. What have you to lose?"

"I don't know—yet!" Conway said. "But there must be a catch in it somewhere. It all sounds too easy."

"There is no catch in it. My principal would like to see you—that is all."

"What have I got that's so unusual—so valuable?"

"Many qualities, Mr. Conway, if you are the man I take you for. Very many qualities. You will learn—if you go to Biarritz."

"Well," Conway said slowly, "it's the strangest thing I ever heard of. . . ." For a moment he studied Venizelos in silence. He could see nothing sinister about him, nothing alarming. The man didn't look in the least like a crook. The eyes behind the gold pince-nez were kindly.

"This principal of yours . . ." Conway said at last. "He must have money to burn."

"That is so," Venizelos agreed. "To you, in your present position, five hundred pounds no doubt seems like wealth. To him, it is—how shall I put it?—a packet of cigarettes."

"It seems incredible." Conway ran a hand through his thick, unruly hair. "Anyway, suppose I said I'd go—when would I get this money?"

"You would get it now," Venizelos said. He looked carefully round the bar. All the customers seemed busy with their own affairs. "I have an envelope in my pocket containing five hundred pounds in English bank notes—and a sheet of paper with all the instructions you will need."

Conway laughed. Incredulity was giving place to excitement. "You must be very sure of yourself."

"I thought it better to come prepared," Venizelos said, with a hint of apology in his voice. "After all, Mr. Conway, it seemed reasonable enough. Here you are, a young, strong, vigorous man, without a job. You have lost your ship, and a chapter in your life has ended. You need money badly. You have already shown that you enjoy living adventurously. And here am I, offering you precisely what you want—a job, money and adventure. All you have to do is step into an airplane. As I said before, what have you to lose?"

Conway said, "May I take a look at the instructions?"

"Of course—but be a little prudent." Venizelos thrust his small ringed hand into the breast pocket of his jacket and drew out a large white envelope, unsealed, which he handed across the table.

Conway glanced inside it. There was a thick wad of bank notes —more than he had ever seen before at one time. There was also a paper with some typing on it. He took it out and read it. It said:

A ROOM IS RESERVED FOR YOU AT THE HOTEL SUPERBE, BIARRITZ. BE AT THE FOOT OF THE LIFT AT BIARRITZ VILLE STATION AT 9 P.M. ON THURSDAY, SEPTEMBER 18, WITH A COPY OF FIGARO IN YOUR LEFT HAND.

"Quite melodramatic!" Conway said, with a grin.

"It is not intended to be. It is just a simple precaution to ensure a reasonable amount of secrecy. . . . Well, Mr. Conway?"

"Well, Mr. Venizelos—perhaps I'm crazy, or perhaps you are —but there's nothing in this place that's holding me back, so I'll take a chance and go. Do you want a receipt for this money?"

"For a packet of cigarettes? I think that is hardly necessary."

"What about my transport?"

13

"I took the liberty," Venizelos said, "of reserving a place for you on the Air France flight that leaves here at three o'clock tomorrow afternoon. The ticket is paid for. You will have to change planes at Paris. It might be a good thing if you called at the Air France office in the morning to give them any particulars they may need. That is all. . . ." He got up, and held out his hand. "It has been a pleasure to meet you, Mr. Conway. I do not think you will come back here, so this is good-by—and good luck!"

He smiled, picked up his hat and cane, and walked primly out of the bar.

Once Venizelos had gone, it became much harder to believe in the bizarre and improbable episode. Several times Conway's hand strayed to his pocket, seeking reassurance that he hadn't been dreaming, that the encounter had actually taken place. But the money was there all right, crisp and comforting. For a while he sat on in a pleasant glow. Whatever happened now, he would get out of Accra. Whatever happened, he would have a little capital to fall back on. His somber outlook had been transformed at a stroke.

Back at the Rest House, the glow persisted. The prospect of meeting Venizelos' principal and learning what he had to propose intrigued him enormously. The slight cloak-and-dagger atmosphere was stimulating. He felt no serious worry about the possibility of danger, since he was not yet committed to anything. For a long while he speculated, enjoyably but fruitlessly, on what the proposition might be. There was so little to go on that he couldn't even make a wild guess. But he continued to mull over it through most of the hot night.

In the morning he put his affairs in order. It still seemed worth while to try and get some of *Tara's* contents back, so he kept his appointment with the contractor and agreed on a figure for the salvage attempt, which he paid. He called at the Air France office and gave his passport particulars, and afterward he went on a shopping spree and re-equipped himself. By three o'clock, when the plane took off, he looked and felt a new man.

In the air, his sense of excitement grew. He had never flown before, and he found it exhilarating. Rushing north across French West Africa gave him an unaccustomed feeling of importance, as though the speed of the aircraft were in some way related to his mission. By the time he reached Paris, he could almost believe that he was engaged on vital business. In *Tara* he had never felt that anything was particularly vital, except to make a landfall in the end. He enjoyed the contrast. He enjoyed the change in the weather, too. In Paris it was hot for September, but Conway found it deliciously cool and dry after the close humidity of Accra. Even Biarritz felt cool when he arrived there on the second evening. He checked in at the Superbe, where a balconied room overlooking the sea had been reserved for him. So far, he reflected, his way could scarcely have been smoother if he had been a visiting potentate. He took a shower, had a leisurely drink in the open-air bar outside the hotel, and dined in sybaritic luxury. Afterward he strolled through the gay, glittering streets, seeing as much of the place as he could in case his visit should be short. At ten minutes to nine he sought directions for Biarritz Ville station, and at nine he was standing at the foot of the lift with a copy of *Figaro* held prominently in his left hand. He had scarcely time to glance around him before a short, burly

15

man approached. "Mr. Conway?" he asked. Conway nodded. "Please!" said the man, and led the way out through the swinging doors. A shiny limousine stood empty at the curb. The man opened the rear door, and Conway climbed in and sank down on the plushy seat.

In a few seconds they were out of the town and running north at high speed along the main coast road. Conway could see little from the car except a confusion of lights, but at some point on the route his eye was caught by a signpost that said "Frontière, 23." That would be the Spanish border, of course. It made him wonder. Was it, perhaps, some smuggling enterprise he was expected to take part in? —or was the proximity of the frontier just an accident? He thought of asking the chauffeur where they were making for, but it seemed hardly worth while. He'd know before long, anyway—and whatever sort of ride he was being taken on, he had no choice but to go through with it now. He sat back. The car sped smoothly on. Very soon they were entering another small town—St.-Jean-de-Luz, the sign said. Almost at once they stopped. Conway caught the glint of water, and against the lights of the surrounding buildings he saw what appeared to be the masts of fishing vessels. The car had pulled up close beside some inner harbor. As he got out another man approached, nodding to the chauffeur. He was wearing a white-topped cap and a white uniform, and looked like a very smart ship's officer. "Quickly, sir, if you please," he said, in an accent that reminded Conway of Venizelos. Conway followed him to the quayside, where an expensive-looking launch lay motionless under the wall. As Conway stepped down, a second uniformed officer touched an engine switch, and in a matter of seconds they were away, passing under a bridge and out of the inner basin. Beyond, there was another basin, leading in turn to a spacious outer harbor. The launch put on speed. Behind them, the town rose splendidly in a great amphitheater of light. Ahead, Conway could make out the masthead lamps and gleaming ports of a ship at anchor. Soon it took shape as a large steam yacht. The launch glided alongside. A white-coated steward was waiting at the top of the steps to usher the visitor aboard. Conway followed him across the deck and down a companionway to a luxuriously appointed saloon. The steward stood back to let him enter, and Conway heard the door close softly behind him.

A short dark man of about Conway's own age advanced quickly to meet him, his hand outstretched. "Mr. Conway!" he said. His handshake was brisk and firm. His brilliant smile suggested more than conventional pleasure. "So my arrangements went smoothly? Good! Well, now, let me introduce myself. . . ." He smiled again, mischievously. "As you spend most of your time at sea, it's quite possible you may not have heard of me. My name is Victor Metaxas."

Conway said "Ah!" drawing out the word. Already, his own presence in St.-Jean-de-Luz seemed less surprising. The casual throwing away—if it should turn out to be that—of five hundred pounds and a two-way air fare was certainly more understandable now. The name of Metaxas was the world's current synonym for riches. Metaxas was one of the big success figures of his generation—a financial prodigy who, from obscure Levantine beginnings, had built up a vast commercial empire and was now reputed to count his wealth in scores of millions. Everyone, everywhere, had heard of Metaxas.

Conway said, "There was a radio on my ship. I always kept up pretty well with the news."

"Excellent!" Metaxas swiveled a chair round for Conway, held out a gold cigarette case, inquired what he would drink, and poured two shots of whisky from a decanter. "It was very good of you to come all this way to see me."

"I had some very material encouragement," Conway said.

Metaxas waved that aside. "I hope you had a good trip."

"A splendid trip, thank you. I'm still rather breathless. Five knots is my kind of speed."

"That's something that makes me quite envious. . . . Well, now, to business. I understand, Mr. Conway, that you are a citizen of the Republic of Eire, and that you hold a southern Irish passport. Is that right?"

"It is."

"Do you consider that you owe any allegiance at all to—England?"

"Indeed I do not."

"Would you have any objection to—shall we say, embarrassing —the British government?"

Conway gave a huge grin. "I'd have no great objection to embarrassing any government!"

"Well, that clears the air. . . . Now let me tell you what's in my mind." Metaxas got up and began to pace to and fro across the saloon. "I am, myself, a native of the island of Spyros. You know, of course, that Spyros is an English colony. You know, too, that for some years it has been engaged in a bitter struggle for its independence."

18

"Sure."

"You've probably heard the name of Alexander Kastella, the political leader of the liberation movement?"

"I have."

"You know that he was arrested by the English some months ago and deported to the island of Heureuse in the Indian Ocean?"

Slowly, Conway nodded.

"Well, Mr. Conway, what I want you to do is sail to Heureuse in your yacht and recover Kastella for us!"

For a moment, Conway just stared. Then he said, "But I have no yacht." It seemed as good a starting point as any.

"A yacht would be provided."

Conway studied the dark, boyishly eager face. "It sounds quite an enterprise!"

"It would be quite an enterprise. Heureuse is a thousand miles from the nearest land. But then you are used to sailing great distances."

"I wasn't thinking of the distance. I was thinking of the very good chance I'd have of spending the next year or two in a British jail. I enjoy my freedom."

"Naturally there would be risks," Metaxas said. "But there would also be danger money. This is my proposition. The moment you agreed to undertake the mission, you would receive a thousand pounds. The day before you sailed you would receive a second thousand pounds. The day you landed Kastella safely at an agreed spot, I would pay a further sum into any bank you cared to name. You would have to trust me over that, but

19

anyone who has done business with me will tell you that I invariably honor my word. The sum I have in mind is—twenty thousand pounds."

Conway looked at him incredulously. "Twenty thousand . . . !"

Metaxas smiled. "When I was a very small boy, Mr. Conway, I used to clean the shoes of tourists outside a hotel in Spyros. Those who paid me the best had the brightest shoes. I am a strong believer in incentives. Judiciously graduated incentives! A little for trying—a lot for succeeding."

"A 'lot' is right," Conway said. "What makes this man Kastella so important?"

"I can tell you that in a few words. Kastella is the only man who can give my country genuine freedom. Since his arrest, the liberation movement has taken a wrong turning. It has got into the hands of unscrupulous and violent men who are using it for their own ends. The British government will never negotiate with them. If they succeeded in gaining independence by force, the outcome could be a worse tyranny than anything we have known. Kastella's return to active control would put the struggle back on the right road, the democratic road—and Spyros would soon be free. That, at least, is my view."

"Twenty thousand pounds seems a great deal to pay for a political view," Conway said.

"Not to me, Mr. Conway. I can assure you I've already paid very much more than that just to publicize the Spyros case throughout the world. Money means very little to me—money for its own sake. It has never been difficult for me to acquire it. I have the Midas touch. Nothing ever seems to go wrong with my ventures. If I take over a shipping concern, inevitably some world crisis develops and there is a shortage of ships. If I start a new airline, my competitors run into a series of misfortunes which bring me traffic. If I buy oil wells, my rivals' pipelines are cut and mine are not. People say I have a flair, an instinct. Perhaps I have. Whatever it is, the money flows in—and I am left with the greatest problem of all: How to spend it with any satisfaction!"

"Yes, I guess that could be a problem," Conway said.

"It has been so for me. One soon tires of personal luxury. Wealth by itself brings no happiness—that is a commonplace. It can have the opposite effect. It can bedevil one's private relationships. I have been married three times, Mr. Conway—three times, and I am not yet forty. Each time I have hoped for success, and found only failure. . . . Of course, I have given a great deal of money away to good causes, but large-scale philanthropy is a remote and unsatisfying thing. The cause of Spyros is different. It is something I can feel about intensely, personally. I should like to be known in history as the man who gave Spyros its freedom. I shall never deserve that, but at least I can play my part, and when Spyros is free, safely and happily free, that freedom will be a memorial to me, as well as to others. . . ." He broke off, smiling a little shyly. "It is only too easy to talk to strangers, Mr. Conway—and I am talking too much. Let us get back to practical matters. What do you think of the enterprise?"

"I couldn't be more dubious about it," Conway said.

"If you weren't dubious at this stage, I should have very little faith in you. . . . But try to be more specific. What exactly are you concerned about?"

21

"Well, in the first place," Conway said, "I doubt if I *could* rescue Kastella. He's bound to be very closely guarded."

"I understand not, Mr. Conway. According to the newspapers, he has very considerable freedom of movement on Heureuse—and why not, since there's nowhere for him to escape to? My guess is that once you had succeeded in contacting him, the rest would be easy." Metaxas smiled. "What the English call 'a piece of cake'!"

"Contacting him might not be easy. Does he speak English?"

"As fluently as I do. Don't forget that English is our second language in Spyros. Besides, he is a highly educated man. He was formerly a lawyer, and a brilliant one."

Conway grunted. "Well, I still see nothing easy about it. . . . Just suppose for the sake of argument that I managed to take him off. They'd send out planes and boats directly they missed him, and we'd be caught in no time."

Metaxas shook his head. "There are no airplanes on Heureuse, Mr. Conway. There is no ground flat enough for an airfield. There is not even a helicopter. There might be a launch or two, but a launch would have great difficulty in finding you. If you left under cover of darkness, I think you would have an excellent chance of getting clean away."

"Where would I make for? You're not suggesting I should try to put him ashore on Spyros?"

"Good gracious, no—the coast is much too well guarded. Smuggling him in would be a major operation, to be carried out later by those who are used to it. . . . No, my suggestion would be that you put him ashore in Kenya, which is the nearest bit of land to Heureuse."

"Another British colony!"

"It sounds unwise, I know, but in fact it would be safer than most places. The coast is very empty, and there's a lot of it. There'd be an element of double bluff—no one would be expecting you to go there. Also, I have people in Mombasa I can rely on—people who would set Kastella on the next stage of his travels. . . . But that is something you needn't bother yourself about, Mr. Conway. Your mission would end at the moment of landing."

Conway grinned. "My troubles wouldn't, though, would they? What would I do afterward?"

"Take up the threads of your adventurous life, I imagine. Roam the oceans once more."

"There'd be a lot of ports I couldn't enter. All the places where the Union Jack flies."

"Well, there aren't as many of those as there used to be, are there?" Metaxas said. "And in much of the world you would be warmly welcomed because of what you had done."

Conway was silent for a while. Then he said, "It's not my line of country, you know. I should think quite a bit of strong-arm stuff might be necessary, and I've no experience of that, and no taste for it, either. What you need for a job like this is an ex-commando."

"What I need is a man of courage, resource and intelligence," Metaxas said, "and I think I've found him. I don't expect you to *fight* your way out of Heureuse. That would be stupid. In any case I wouldn't want it—there's been far too much bloodshed already for the good of our cause. I would hope for a skillful and silent departure."

23

"All the same, there must be many men better equipped than I am."

"On the contrary," Metaxas said, "you are the first man I have come across who, in my view, could undertake the mission with any hope of success. Obviously, the rescuer must be a yachtsman—any larger expedition would be sure to arouse suspicion. There are, of course, other ocean-going yachtsmen, but . . ." Metaxas smiled ". . . if you'll forgive my saying so, Mr. Conway, most men who sail the oceans singlehanded are somewhat eccentric—which means that most of them, in fact, are Englishmen! Naturally, no Englishman of any caliber would look at my proposition. I've been thinking about a possible rescue operation ever since Kastella was interned, and I've actually made considerable preparations against the eventuality, but it wasn't until I heard about you from my agent, Venizelos, that I saw any real hope. If you refuse my mission, I think it most likely I shall have to drop the idea altogether. That is why I have talked to you so freely, even before you have committed yourself in any way. It is now, or never."

Again, Conway fell silent. Presently he said, "You say that a rescue would be impossible with anything larger than a yacht, because suspicion would be aroused. But what makes you think the authorities wouldn't be suspicious of a yacht? There can't be many of them arriving in Heureuse waters—especially yachts flying the flag of Eire. If you ask me, the moment the police set eyes on that, they'd double the guard until I left. They'd be pretty stupid if they didn't."

"It's a good point," Metaxas said, "and one that I'd already thought of. It would be advisable, I think, for you to sail under the British flag."

"I'd as soon sail under the skull and crossbones!" Conway said, with a grin. "Anyway, what about my Irish passport?"

"You'd have to have a United Kingdom passport, of course, in a different name."

"You mean you could arrange that!"

"I can arrange almost anything," Metaxas said, "except the freeing of Alexander Kastella by the British government. The passport would be a very simple matter. You could be from Ulster. That would account for your slight brogue—and Ulstermen are considered even more British than the English, are they not?"

Conway gave a preoccupied nod. "All the same, I still think the authorities on Heureuse would be suspicious of a yacht that arrived without any particular reason. I'd need some good story to disarm them, some cover, something to satisfy them that the visit was an innocent one."

"That would certainly help," Metaxas agreed. "We must look into it. Some scientific purpose, perhaps . . ."

"Anyway," Conway said, "what about the boat?"

"It is waiting for you. I am the owner—though it's not in my name, of course—of a small yacht lying now in Mombasa harbor. My associate there picked it out for me when I first became interested in the possibility of an expedition. Its name is *Thalia*. Would you care to see the plans?"

"Indeed I would."

Metaxas fetched some papers from a bureau and spread them

25

out on the table. There were drawings and photographs and specifications. Conway studied them all carefully. The examination took him quite a time.

"Well," he said at last, "she certainly seems like a nice little ship."

"She would be yours at the end of the mission," Metaxas told him. "I would throw her in—as an extra."

Conway smiled grimly. "You make it all sound so attractive, so tempting. But I can tell you one thing right away. This ship would be quite unsuitable."

Metaxas looked startled. "Why do you say that?"

"She'd be hopeless as a singlehander," Conway said. "My own ship, *Tara*, was a Bermudan yawl, rather old-fashioned, with a deep forefoot and a long straight keel. She'd sail herself on pretty well any point of the wind. This ship is a sloop, and by the lines of her I'd say she'd need someone at the tiller practically all the time. Look at her cutaway bow—she'd never sail herself with the wind aft. I'd have to be constantly heaving to to get any sleep—and I doubt if she'd lie very comfortably hove to, either. The trip might take weeks. In fact, I simply wouldn't undertake an ocean voyage in her singlehanded—not as she is now."

"Couldn't she be altered?" Metaxas asked anxiously.

"She could, I dare say—she could have a mizzen stepped, for one thing. But in Mombasa the job would probably take months —the adapting, and the trials, and the re-adapting. It's a long job, getting a boat just right for ocean sailing. . . . Maybe there's another boat in some other convenient port—one that wouldn't need so much altering."

"There may well be," Metaxas said, "but finding it could also

26

take months, and there's no time to lose. . . ." He looked thoughtfully at Conway. "Perhaps the best way out would be for you to take someone else with you."

Conway gave a dubious shrug. "It would get over the sailing problem, of course, but I've always preferred being alone at sea. Quarters are pretty cramped in a small yacht, and I'm not the easiest man to get on with. . . . Besides, could you find anyone else?"

"Would your companion have to be a skilled yachtsman, too?"

"Not necessarily. It would help if he knew the difference between land and water, but it might be better if he wasn't too knowledgeable—there'd be less chance of a squabble! He'd have to be able to steer the boat when I was asleep, that's all, and be generally useful and cheerful around the place. He'd soon pick up all he needed to know if he was the right type."

"In that case," Metaxas said, "I think I may be able to produce someone suitable. I shall certainly do my best. . . . What I suggest, Mr. Conway, is that you go back now to your hotel. Don't attempt to get in touch with me tomorrow—it's better that we should appear to have no contact with each other. Tomorrow evening at—let me see—seven o'clock exactly, be in the open-air bar outside the Superbe. At that hour, with any luck, my candidate will call on you to be interviewed. The name, by the way, is Sophoulis."

"Very well," Conway said. "I hope you understand, though, that I'm not committing myself in any way about the enterprise. I owe you something for that five hundred pounds and I'll certainly have a look at your man, but frankly I think the whole thing's quite crazy and I can't see myself undertaking it."

27

"It's possible," Metaxas said with a smile, "that the idea may grow on you."

Conway spent most of the next day sitting out on the end of the great breakwater, quietly weighing the pros and cons of Metaxas' proposition. It still seemed fairly crazy, looked at as a whole, but there were aspects that appealed to him. He had been very much taken by the sloop *Thalia*. He had never sailed across that part of the Indian Ocean. He would enjoy visiting Heureuse. He had nothing against giving the British lion's tail an additional tweak. If it proved impracticable to take Kastella off, he would still be two thousand pounds to the good—and success would give him all the money he could ever use. That was the credit side. The dangers were equally obvious. The passport offense alone, if discovered, would be enough to jail him. An unsuccessful attempt at rescue might cost him years of freedom. Physical damage to himself could certainly not be ruled out.

He had reached no decision by the evening, except that it would be foolish to turn the offer down out of hand. Much would depend on this fellow Sophoulis, whom Metaxas, in his dynamic way, was no doubt whisking from some distant part of the globe. If he turned out to be congenial, it would be hard to say "No."

The hotel bar was fairly active when Conway went down at a quarter to seven. He stood for a moment surveying the tables. At the far end the customers were thinner on the ground; there was a French family, laughing and chattering, an old man in a Basque beret, a girl on her own reading a book, and a younger man, thickset and sturdy looking, also on his own. Conway wondered if he was Sophoulis. At present he seemed to be concentrating on trying to catch the eye of the girl.

Conway chose a table well away from all of them, and ordered a Dubonnet, and waited. Seven o'clock struck. People drifted in and out. Conway inspected each new arrival closely, but no one approached his table or showed any interest in him. Five past seven. Ten past. For once, Metaxas' machinelike arrangements seemed to have gone awry. Perhaps he hadn't been able to get hold of his man—but in that case surely he would have sent a message? Seven-fifteen. Conway continued to watch and wait. Presently the young man abandoned his attempts to pick up the girl, and left. Almost at once, the girl closed her book and came over to Conway's table.

"Good evening," she said. "Are you Mr. Michael Conway?"

"I am."

"My name is Sophoulis. Leanda Sophoulis. Victor Metaxas sent me."

Conway nearly dropped his glass. "Oh—*no!*"

"I was afraid it might be rather a shock. . . . Do you mind if I join you?" Her English was accentless and perfect.

Mechanically, Conway waved her to a chair. "Metaxas must be out of his mind!"

"He's not usually thought to be," the girl said. "Most people think he's extremely clever."

"He may be a clever financier, but this is positively schoolboyish. . . . He's just a frustrated romantic."

"He thinks I should make a suitable companion for you. So do I."

"But it's absurd. . . ." Conway broke off, studying her. She was small, almost fragile to look at, but exquisitely shaped. Her

29

little head was set in a halo of smooth black hair. Her face was a delicate miniature, with beautifully marked eyebrows and long lashes. Her dark, spirited eyes, set slightly on the slant, matched the resolution of her small chin. She was, Conway had to admit, a most unusual-looking girl. He put her age at twenty-three or twenty-four.

"Who are you, anyway?" he said. "How do you come into this?"

"I work for Victor. I help with his propaganda—I have an office in Paris. He rang me there last night, and I flew in today."

Conway grinned. "Well, now you'll have to fly out again! You surely don't expect me to take this idea seriously?"

"Why not?"

"I can think of a dozen reasons. . . . Have you ever been in a small boat at sea?"

"No, but you told Victor it wasn't necessary for your crew to have expert knowledge. I'm certain I could learn to steer. Don't forget we're a seafaring people in Spyros."

"Have you the slightest idea what it's like to make an ocean passage in a small yacht?"

"I imagine it can be very uncomfortable."

"Uncomfortable! It can be absolute hell. Rough, tough— terrifying. Until you've tried it, you can have no conception. For days on end you get tossed about like a cork. You can't eat properly, you can't sleep properly. . . . There are times when you almost wish you were dead."

"*You* seem to like it, Mr. Conway."

"I like it and I hate it—but at least I'm used to it. You're not."

"I've read of women who got used to it, and did very well."

"Maybe, but you're not the type. You're a very attractive girl, Miss Sophoulis, and I'd be happy to take you dancing any time. But sailing . . ." He shook his head. "Look at your dainty hands. After two weeks at sea they'd be so cut and callused you wouldn't recognize them. Your body would probably be black and blue. You'd be so seasick you'd want to throw yourself overboard. When it was too late, you'd wish you hadn't come. So would I. Far from being a help, you'd be a burden."

"I never have been seasick," Leanda said, "although I've traveled by sea quite a lot. If I were, I should try not to be a burden. You mustn't judge too much by appearances, you know—I'm actually very tough. In any case, you don't have to make up your mind about me now. If we went to Mombasa together, you'd have plenty of time to get to know me before we started. You could always turn me down if I wasn't any good."

Conway regarded her wonderingly. "Just exactly in what capacity would you plan to travel with me?"

"I discussed that with Victor," she said coolly. "We think it would be better if I came as your wife."

Conway grinned. "You mean you're offering to marry me?"

"Don't be absurd. . . . I mean as your notional wife, that's all."

"H'm!" Conway leaned back with his head on one side. "Well, n some ways it's quite a notion!"

"I'm serious, Mr. Conway, and I wish you would be. I don't egard any part of this as a joke—I'm in deadly earnest. Surely ou can see that the advantages of my coming with you would e enormous? If I were with you, as your wife, the authorities n Heureuse would have no suspicions at all. It would merely seem like a holiday trip. I don't believe you could have a better cover."

Conway looked at her thoughtfully. "Yes, there may be something in that. . . . All the same, it staggers me that you're willing to contemplate it. You don't know me at all—I'm a complete stranger to you. Wouldn't you be taking rather a chance—putting yourself completely in my hands, even to the extent of being a notional wife?"

"To me," Leanda said, "that aspect is not very important."

"It might be to me. Suppose I turned out to be the worst kind of wolf?"

Leanda smiled. "It seems unlikely, since you choose to spend most of your time alone at sea. Besides, you would find me very uninteresting from that point of view. My mind is entirely occupied with other things."

"What other things?"

"My country, above everything."

"A dedicated woman, eh?"

"I suppose it sounds unnatural," Leanda said, "but it's true. In Spyros, where I grew up, we all think more of freedom than of anything else. Why *should* the English rule us? We are a proud people, Mr. Conway—we had a civilization in Spyros when the English were still living in caves. Yet they treat us as though we were aborigines. To be always subordinate and inferior in your own country—that is intolerable."

Conway nodded slowly. "All right—you put your country first. That still doesn't equip you for a hard, dangerous mission."

"You talk as though I were a delicate little flower, Mr. Conway —as though I'd lived a very sheltered life. I assure you nothing

32

could be further from the truth. I spent three months in an English prison in Spyros—for distributing illegal literature. I have also been beaten up in the street by the police. But that was really nothing. . . . Two of my friends, two boys still in their teens, were *hanged* a year ago. And even that is not the worst. I have seen terrible things happen—things I wish I could forget. . . . So you see, I am *not* a little flower."

"Maybe it was a hasty judgment," Conway said. He was silent for a moment. "What had your two friends done?"

"They threw bombs. They considered themselves at war."

"Have you thrown bombs?"

"No. I'm against violence and terror. Its results are too horrible."

"I agree with you. . . . What was that particularly frightful thing I heard on the radio while I was at sea—a description of some village where three young men who wouldn't join your movement were mutilated and killed, as a lesson to others. Perhaps that wasn't true. I don't know."

"It was true. It was in Meos. I wasn't in Spyros then—I'd been forced to leave because the police wanted me again, and I was already working for Victor—but I know it was true. It was the most ghastly thing that has happened—almost unbelievable. . . . There has been so much killing and being killed, so much hate and misery. I can understand that, to some people, violence seems the only way. The English have been so stupid and smug and deaf to argument. But I'm sure it's wrong. My friends who were hanged were brave, so brave, but I think they were wrong, too. I think that real freedom will only come through reason and negotiation—however long it may take. And that, as Victor told you, is why we need Kastella."

Conway said, "Do you know Kastella? Have you met him?"

"I met him once," she said, her dark eyes lighting up. "The struggle was just beginning. I'd helped to organize a meeting for him, and afterward he shook hands with me. He is a fine, humane man, and a wonderful leader. He hates violence—he worked in the Resistance against the Nazis during the last war and saw more than enough of it then. He is clever and farsighted and patient. Once he is free, he will end the terror—he will negotiate a settlement, and the English will go. Then we shall have a peaceful and happy country again."

Conway said, "H'm!"

"You sound unsympathetic, Mr. Conway—yet you are an Irishman; you should understand what it feels like to live under the English."

"In Ireland," Conway said, "that was a bit before my time. I can't say I've any personal grudge against the English. There are no martyrs in my family."

"But you can't have any love for them."

"I wouldn't say I'd any love for them, no. I don't like the way they're always pushing other people around from the highest moral motives. I don't like being pushed around myself, and I don't like pushers. So I'm with you most of the way—I can quite understand why you want to get rid of them. Anyway, all countries want to run their own affairs—it's natural."

"Then why did you look so cynical just now?"

"You were so sure that everything would be fine afterward. You're an idealist, Miss Sophoulis, you have belief and faith. Free Kastella, you say, and then we shall have a peaceful and

34

happy country. Then, everything will be all right. But it never is. Often, it's worse. Slavery can be comfortable and freedom can be hell. The dreams never come true."

"One can always hope."

"Oh, sure. . . . What I'm trying to say is that our angles on this thing are different. If I did decide to go off on this crazy mission, it wouldn't be because I thought I was doing a great service to someone or making people any happier."

"You mean it would be for the money."

"For the money, and only for the money. I'd be a mercenary, and that would have to be quite clear from the start. Not that I think I'd ever need twenty thousand pounds, but I could certainly use a fine ship."

"Does that mean so much to you?"

"It means pretty well everything to me. It's my way of life."

"Aren't you ever lonely?"

"Oh, yes, sometimes, when the weather's good and there's not much to occupy me. But the feeling passes."

"What's attractive about the life?"

"To me? Absolute freedom and independence. Never having to study anyone's wishes but my own."

"It sounds selfish, the way you put it."

"Maybe it is—but I can't help that. I ask very little of the world and I don't think I owe it anything. At least, the way I live doesn't harm anybody else."

"But surely," Leanda said, "one has to *do* something in the world. Not just go round and round it."

"I don't see why. It seems to me there are far too many people doing far too much already. Wasn't it Lord Melbourne who once

35

said, 'Whenever I hear a man say something must be done, I know he's about to do something damn silly!'? I prefer just going round and round."

"But one can't live happily without responsibility or friends or affection."

"I get by," Conway said. "I'm used to traveling light. There's all the responsibility I want getting my ship safely to port. And I have a lot of friends round the world, even though I don't look them up very often—or perhaps because!"

"Don't you ever get bored?"

"Not for long—the contrasts are too sharp for that. When I've been at sea for a week or two I can't bear the sight of it and long for the shore. Then I go ashore, and I enjoy it much more than most landsmen, I can tell you. When I've been ashore for a few days I can't bear the sight of that either. So I go to sea again, and it feels marvelous."

"It all sounds very pointless," Leanda said.

"What isn't?"

"In my view, freeing Alexander Kastella."

Conway laughed. "Well, we seem to be back where we started. You're dedicated—I'm not. At least we have no illusions about each other—which is just as well if we're to go along together for a bit."

Her eyes opened wide. "You mean we *are* to go along together?"

"We'll go to Mombasa, anyway," Conway said, "and see what happens."

"That was a remarkably quick decision."

"Well, you're rather a remarkable woman," Conway said.

FOR LEANDA

It took five days for the initial arrangements to be made. In that time, Conway and Leanda paid several secret visits to the anchored steam yacht after dark. Metaxas, exuberantly pleased at Conway's decision, threw himself eagerly into the preliminary planning. The details, he agreed, would have to be settled by Conway in Mombasa, but he hoped to get a steady flow of coded information from there through his agent, a man named Ionides, with whom Conway would be working. He still tended to talk of the prospective expedition as though it were a rather glamorous adventure, but there was no denying his shrewd grasp of all the practical questions involved. He was, Conway could see, a brilliant organizer of immense energy, and his pleasure at being able to use his talents in an active way on behalf of Spyros was unmistakable. Until now, Conway suspected, he had been little more in the politics of his country than a keen and well-meaning amateur, naïvely pretending to himself that he was at the heart of the struggle when in fact he was out of touch and operating in a wordy vacuum of his own on the periphery. Now, beyond any doubt, he was doing something that could have a tremendous effect on his country's future.

Conway saw a good deal of Leanda during the five days' wait, and his admiration for her steadily increased. She was intense where Spyros was concerned, and very single-minded, but she wasn't in the least strident. Having made her position plain, she showed no tendency to dwell on her country's wrongs, and any fear Conway might have had that he'd have to listen to a lot of tedious harangues proved quite unfounded. Her main interest now, like his own, appeared to be a practical one. He managed to find out a little more about her—that her father had been a

37

well-to-do businessman with a cosmopolitan background and no politics; that she had been educated at an English school in Switzerland, which accounted for her lack of a Spyros accent; that both her parents were now dead. But she talked about her personal life only when he questioned her, and then briefly. Their relationship was that of a working partnership, and Leanda clearly meant to keep it that way.

By the sixth day, all was ready, and they flew off to Paris with a stack of brand-new luggage appropriate to a young couple who had recently married, and a credit in Conway's bank totaling nearly fifteen hundred pounds. In Paris they made the notional change-over to the married state and picked up two United Kingdom passports from an address that Metaxas had given them. One, a rather battered one, was in the name of Michael Cornford, gentleman, born in Belfast, with a photograph—skillfully made to look old—that Conway had had taken in St.-Jean-de-Luz for the purposes of the forgery. The other was new and shiny, the property of Leanda Cornford, née Owen, born in Bangor, Wales. The Welsh touch had been Conway's idea—it might help to explain, he thought, Leanda's distinctly exotic type of loveliness. Both passports were stamped with a false entry into France via Calais a fortnight before. Both were works of art. Conway hoped they would also prove serviceable, since he was now committed for the first time in his life to a considerable illegality. It was all very well for Leanda, he said teasingly, as they took off from Paris on the Kenya flight—she was already an old lag! But he felt no real anxiety—their front was a good one. Who would be suspicious of a young, wealthy, and highly presentable couple who were flying to Mombasa to look at a yacht they'd seen advertised, with the idea of spending the bleak English winter cruising under romantic tropic skies? "All the world loves a lover," Conway said. Leanda had learned to smile at cracks like that. She didn't really approve of his tendency to mock, any more than she approved of his blatant mercenariness, but as long as he got on with the job she didn't mind.

They changed planes at Nairobi and reached Mombasa in the evening of the second day. There they drove to the Ambassadors, a five-star hotel on Prince Charles Street where an elegant suite had been reserved for them. Only one of the rooms was equipped as a bedroom, but the suite was spacious—much more spacious, Conway said with a grin, than *Thalia* would be! He found the unusual situation amusing and intriguing. Leanda, as she had said she would, took it completely in her stride. Her public attitude had been affectionate; now that they were alone together she was coolly businesslike and detached. Conway was much more aware of her physically than she was of him. As he climbed into one of the twin beds, he was reminded of those matter-of-fact young women whom agencies provide to spend innocent nights with prospective divorcees. Any kind of pass would have seemed a breach of taste, as well as of contract. In fact, they both slept well in the deep privacy of mosquito nets.

First thing in the morning Conway telephoned their contact, Ionides, who ran the Transport and General Mercantile Company in Mombasa. The agent said he'd come straight over, and he turned up in a Cadillac just after ten, smoking a huge cigar. He was an enormously fat, physically lethargic man, with a paunch like a bass drum. Conway liked him at once. There was nothing lethargic about his twinkling dark eyes or his quick

39

intelligence, and it soon became clear that he had the whole
situation very much in hand. He was, it appeared, Metaxas' agent
only in the personal and political sense. The two had known each
other in boyhood and had kept in touch; they shared the same
attitudes over Spyros and the same hopes of Kastella; and when
Ionides had learned that *Thalia* was for sale he'd snapped her
up, ostensibly on his own account. Everything had been done
discreetly, and the close association between him and Metaxas
was not generally known in Mombasa, so that Conway and Leanda could deal with the agent openly.

They had a short talk, and then Ionides took them to lunch
at his pleasant veranda'd bungalow above the golf links, where
he introduced them to his pretty dark wife and five of his eight
children. After a siesta he got out plans and maps so that Conway could study the city and its surroundings. Mombasa, Conway discovered, was built largely on an island, which was linked
on the northwest. Round the island flowed a wide and sheltered
creek, deep and safe, providing along one arm the old harbor
of Mombasa, now almost entirely given up to Arab dhows, and
along another the modern harbor of Kilindini, where the great
ships berthed. Southward, between the two harbors, lay a broad
lagoon, and beyond, the narrow exit through the reef to the
Indian Ocean. *Thalia*—which they would now go and look at,
Ionides said—was lying hauled out above an inlet called
Mbaraki Creek, not far from the Yacht Club. A few minutes later
they were on their way in the Cadillac.

Conway, judging his prospective ship as sailors do, by "a blow
in the eye," had an immediately favorable impression. Her lines,
as he'd already learned from the drawing, were modern, but

40

not exaggeratedly so, and he guessed she would be reasonably comfortable and sea-kindly, without being slow. Even out of her element she made a lovely picture, with her dazzling white hull, her impeccable mahogany brightwork, her chromium fittings and instruments. A rich man's toy, Conway thought—though none the worse for that. He walked slowly round her, not wishing to hurry the first pleasurable impact. The draught was about five feet, which should give her a good grip of the water. Judging by the size of the lead keel, most of the ballast was outside. He stroked the immaculate copper sheathing with appreciative fingers—no teredo worm would bore through that.

Presently he followed Leanda up the short ladder to the cockpit. Aboard, he carried out a thorough examination. The ship was obviously in excellent condition, practically new. There was no need here to probe with a knife for dry rot. She was strong, too—many of the oak frames, he saw, were doubled. The joinery was a delight, the teak deck round the coach roof beautifully laid. With her thirty feet of length and nine feet of beam, her accommodation seemed spacious after *Tara's*—a main saloon, with a fixed table between two settee berths and all modern conveniences leading off it; an open cockpit aft; and a forecabin with one bunk. The galley at the after end of the saloon, with its stainless-steel-covered bench and swinging two-burner paraffin stove, left nothing to be desired. There was a roomy navigation space with a chart table and drawers below full of admiralty charts—including, Conway noted, a complete set for the Indian Ocean. He examined the food bins, the ventilators, the chain locker. He took a look at the carefully stowed sails, noting with approval that they were all tanned and proofed

41

against mildew. Back on deck he inspected the halyards and the sheets, the winches and guard rails and steel-tube pulpit forward, the laced canvas dodgers for the cockpit, the anchors and the chain, and the tiny alloy pram dinghy on the coach roof. He opened up the engine—a Diesel in fine condition which he reckoned would give *Thalia* at least eight knots. It seemed unnecessarily powerful for such a yacht, but the speed might well come in useful. He checked the various tanks aboard and found them all full of Diesel fuel, none of water, except for a five-gallon emergency tank. The water supply was by means of a filter-and-chemical apparatus, which could change salt water into fresh as it was wanted. Conway had used a similar apparatus himself ever since it had first come on the market, and had found it wholly satisfactory.

He finished his survey and stood by the tiller, looking forward with absorbed delight. He had loved *Tara*, but she hadn't been in *Thalia's* class. This ship was the stuff of dreams. Now that he had seen her he felt sure she could be altered to make her a good ocean singlehander. It would take time, but that was something he usually had plenty of. Already he could see himself resuming his travels in her—if only he could carry out Metaxas' mission successfully. . . .

Presently he became aware of Leanda beside him. She had barely spoken to him during his tour of inspection. Now, as anxious as a patient waiting for the doctor's verdict, she said, "What do you think of her, Mike?"

"What do *you*?" Conway asked, smiling.

"She's luxurious—wonderful. But will she do?"

"Ah," Conway said, "it's a bit early to tell you that. Let's go and talk to Ionides about launching her."

The agent was sleeping in the car, but he woke at the sound of their voices. "Well?" he said.

"She seems to be just about all set for an ocean voyage. Who did she belong to?"

"An English accountant. He had her sent out from England just before he retired. He was going to sail her to Mauritius. He was full of plans. Then he had a heart attack, and he had to sell her."

"What a shame!" Leanda said.

Conway was still looking at *Thalia*. "She's a lovely ship."

"She cost nearly three thousand pounds," Ionides said.

"Well, if her performance is anything like her promise I'd say you got her at a knockdown price. . . . There's only one change I would suggest, that we could make in the time. That white paint's a bit bright."

"Too visible on a dark night?"

Conway nodded. "We might have to go over it with something else. . . . Anyway, when can I take her out?"

"Tomorrow afternoon," Ionides said. "I'll arrange for her to be put in the water for you in the morning."

The southeaster, that blew constantly from the sea at that time of year, was of moderate strength when Conway and Leanda returned to *Thalia* next day. "A perfect sailing breeze!" Conway said, in visibly high spirits. The day was sunny, and far too warm for comfort on the land, but he guessed that afloat it would be just right. He was wearing a bush shirt, and khaki shorts, which he had always found the most serviceable for

43

tropical sailing. Leanda also wore shorts. "The only possible wear in a boat for a woman of virtue!" he had told her with a grin.

Afloat, the little ship looked even more attractive than it had the previous day. "The loveliest thing man ever invented," Conway said poetically, "a sailing ship." He stood looking at her for a moment in an attitude almost of worship. Then he got busy. Leanda sat by the tiller, watching him as he sorted out what seemed to her a hopeless tangle of sheets and halyards. She was beginning to doubt if she would ever be very useful, but at least she could keep out of his way, and she found him interesting to watch. The mere act of boarding the ship seemed to have given him added stature. His lined, rugged face was no longer mocking, but absorbed. His strong brown hands moved among the ropes with confidence. His well-muscled arms served him with a practiced economy of effort. All his movements were unhurried—so much so that Leanda grew impatient at his deliberation. But at last he gave the signal, and the two smiling Negroes from the boat yard cast off the lines, which he coiled in a leisurely fashion as *Thalia* blew gently away from the shore. Then he hoisted the big red mainsail and they bore away toward Kilindini.

They sailed down past the docks, where cars and cement and agricultural machinery were being unloaded from huge ships onto scorching wharves. They sailed along the edge of mangrove swamps, where the low glaucous trees threw out branches that curved down into the mud like flying buttresses. They turned and sailed almost to the reef, with its piled-up masses of blue-green water and its crests of foam. They sailed past a pink cliff-like pile known as Fort Jesus, and right through the old harbor, where Arab dhows with great triangular sails and wonderfully carved stems and sterns were unloading Persian rugs and Mangalore tiles, and naked Negroes with splendid torsos were fishing with nets, waist-deep in crystal water at the edges of the creek.

The trials lasted for three hours. In that time Conway tested *Thalia* on every point of sailing, experimenting constantly with the sheets and the tiller, seeing how she lay hove-to, judging her speed on a reach, beating out across the south of the lagoon in an exhilarating cloud of spray and seeing how she came about in the swell, first on one tack and then on the other, and how she took the seas as they came up under her stern. Sometimes he told Leanda what he was doing; once he asked her if she felt seasick, and she said no. Most of the time he was silent, and she asked no questions. When he had finished with the sails he started the engine and they cruised up and down for another hour, testing *Thalia's* speed under power and getting a rough idea of the fuel consumption. But the engine was noisy, and Conway switched it off in the end with relief. "Horrible things!" he said.

It was after five when they tied up, and a clammy sea mist was beginning to creep in, making the air seem chill. Even then, Conway hadn't finished. With Leanda's help, he put the pram dinghy in the water and they went for a short row round the anchorage. The dinghy, with two people in it, had very little freeboard, but it would be safe enough in smooth water.

As they rowed back to *Thalia*, Leanda couldn't restrain herself any longer.

"Won't you stop being a sphinx now," she said, "and tell me whether she'll do?"

"Oh, yes," Conway said, "she'll do."

"You mean you'll take her to Heureuse?"

"I'll never have a better chance of getting a boat like this of my own."

"And what about me?" she asked anxiously. "You can't say I got in the way. Will I do?"

"The thing is," he said, in his old bantering tone, "would you be a congenial companion?"

"Mike, please!"

He looked at her eager face. "I reckon you'll do," he said. "We'll go and tell Ionides the trip's on."

The agent was scarcely less delighted than Leanda over Conway's decision. That evening he arranged for the dispatch of a coded message to Metaxas telling him the news. Afterward he raised the crucially important question of where Kastella would be put ashore, supposing the expedition were successful. The harbor at Mombasa, he said, though comparatively easy to find and enter, was under too close supervision to make it suitable for a secret landing from a yacht—and Conway agreed. A much better place, Ionides thought, was a small town called Malindi, some forty miles up the coast to the north. It was a holiday resort, popular on weekends because there was a wide gap in the reef there and the surf bathing was good, but almost deserted on weekdays. Ionides himself had a holiday shack just outside the town, which might be very useful. He suggested that Conway and Leanda should go with him next day to do a bit of reconnoitering.

First thing in the morning, therefore, they set off northward in the Cadillac. There was a fair amount of traffic on the route, but between the road and the sea the flat coastal belt seemed sparsely populated. There were one or two attractive coastal villages—groups of square, palm-thatched houses built of coconut poles plastered with coral mud, where innumerable small children played in the sand and girls, naked to the waist and wearing moplike kilts of grass around their hips, tilled small cassava plots and patches of sweet corn. Otherwise there was little to be seen but the featureless maze of the palm trees that rattled their stiff dark plumes against the blue-green background of the sea. The Cadillac was checked several times by sluggish creeks that ran deep inland between banks thick with foliage. Primitive ferries, worked by gangs of men hauling on ropes, carried the car slowly across, with much chanting and stamping of feet and songs that included improvised compliments to the passengers. It was nearly twelve before they reached Malindi. Once there, Ionides led the way straight to the beach, so that Conway could see for himself what the approach from the sea was like. A quarter of a mile from the shore, the gap in the reef was clearly visible—a stretch of unbroken water several cables wide. As the rollers came surging in over the shallows, they broke in white-capped waves with a loud, incessant roar. No dinghy would live in that kind of sea. But to right and left of the opening, where the reef acted as a breakwater, the lagoon was almost motionless.

"What do you think of it?" Ionides asked.

"Quite good," Conway said after a moment, "provided the weather's calm outside. . . . What's the depth of water in the lagoon?"

"It is shallow, but never less than six feet."

47

"Are you sure of that?"

"I am quite sure—I have fished here many times."

Conway nodded. "Then I could bring *Thalia* through the gap and anchor her in the lee of the reef, out of the surf. From there it would be an easy row."

"Could you find the gap at night?"

"With a bit of luck, I could. Surf always shows up well. I won't say it wouldn't be tricky, but anything's going to be tricky on this coast."

Ionides laid an approving hand on Conway's shoulder. "Good! Now I will show you my shack, and tell you the plan I have thought of."

They turned to the right along the shore, skirting the seaward edge of the trees. Among the elephant-gray trunks of the palms, dozens of tiny holiday huts were dotted. Most of them were of wood and thatch. A few were more permanent concrete bungalows of a modest type. After a quarter of a mile or so the huts began to thin out. The last one of all was Ionides'—a white-painted, veranda'd wooden shack, on a concrete base, set deep among the trees and backing on to a sandy track scored with wheel marks. The name on the gate was *Stella*. The agent took a key from under a pot beside the door and led the way in. There were two small rooms, with some light holiday furniture and a lot of seaside equipment.

"Just a bathing hut, you see," Ionides said. "Now this is what I would suggest. You would bring the yacht inside the reef and row Kastella ashore, as you said. You would set him down a little further along the beach than this, perhaps two hundred yards further, where there are no huts. You yourself would return immediately to the yacht, without landing, and put to sea. The most important thing of all is that no one should see the yacht, for otherwise there might be questions. Your last task would be to disappear quickly. Kastella would walk to his right, along the beach. The first bungalow would be mine. It would be locked, but the key is always kept under that pot, and you would have told him about it. On the table, I would have left money for a telephone call. At daybreak, or just before, he would continue along the track to the right. After four hundred yards, there is a telephone box. He would ring me up at my home. I would have left my telephone number with the money. In a couple of hours I would collect him in my car. Very soon after that I would have put him secretly aboard one of our ships for Europe. . . . How does that strike you, Mr. Conway?"

"It all sounds most efficient," Conway said. "Of course, I can't give you any idea when to expect us. It could be four weeks, six weeks, eight weeks—there's no telling. You'd have to stay put in Mombasa."

"I shall stay until I hear from Kastella, or until I learn that the expedition has failed. I think everything will go quite smoothly. In any case, Kastella will be in no immediate danger once he is ashore. No one knows him here. If anything went wrong with the arrangements, he could take a bus into Mombasa and come to my house. The telephone call is merely a simpler and quicker way of arranging transport."

Conway nodded. Presently he walked down the beach to the water's edge, and turned, and studied the shape of the trees against the sky, memorizing the outline. Against the stars, it would look much the same. And Ionides' shack, a blotch of white among the palms, would help to guide him in.

"All right," he said, as he rejoined the others. "Malindi it is!"

All that remained now was to make the final preparations for the voyage, and Conway and Leanda threw themselves with zest into the task. *Thalia's* inventory of spares and equipment was already so comprehensive that Conway had only to check through it and make sure there were no gaps. But there were large quantities of tinned provisions to be ordered and stowed—sufficient to give an ample margin of safety for three. Day by day *Thalia* sank lower in the water, and still there were things to be remembered. It was Leanda who pointed out that Kastella might well join them with no more than the clothes he was wearing, and that he would need all sorts of things for the journey back. She made a list—"comforts for Our Leader," Conway called them, with an irreverent chuckle. They covered everything, from razor and toothbrush to a broad-brimmed hat, and Conway did that part of the shopping, ostensibly for himself. For the first time in his sailing career, too, he equipped himself with tropical evening clothes, matching Leanda's smart dresses, so that they would be able to take part, if necessary, in Heureuse's social life. He also bought a varied pile of books, to replace those he had lost in *Tara*, and a double-barreled, twelve-bore shotgun, also a replacement. "I was once attacked by a spearfish," he told Leanda, "a horrible brute nearly ten feet long, with a three-foot spear that would have gone through *Tara's* hull like butter! I've always carried a shotgun since then." Leanda looked at him a little disbelievingly, but she let it pass.

There were other things to do besides getting supplies aboard.

FOR LEANDA

With a slight feeling of regret, Conway had *Thalia's* white hull repainted a deep turquoise, explaining to the boat yard that he couldn't stand the glare. As soon as the paint was dry he began to take Leanda out and give her sailing lessons. She showed no special aptitude but she was very determined and it wasn't long before he felt that he could safely leave her at the tiller in good weather. Ashore, they both behaved as though they were about to set out on an exciting holiday trip. The act was necessary, for by now there was a good deal of local interest in their plans. Ionides had already introduced them to the Yacht Club, of which he was an honorary member—it would be thought very odd, he said, if they didn't mix with the local enthusiasts. There were one or two anxious moments, as members politely probed Conway's sailing background and he had to invent imaginary cruises and give the name of an imaginary club in Belfast and appear competent without being in any way unique. Ionides stood watchfully by, ready to intervene if things became too difficult, but the danger passed and the visitors were soon accepted with friendship and encouragement and much good advice. Their story was accepted, too—that they were bound for the Seychelles, and hoped to come back via Mauritius. No one seemed to find the project unreasonable in a ship like *Thalia*. After a few convivial drinking sessions, Conway was able to plead pressure of preparations and stay away from the club.

In just over a fortnight they were ready. On the last night but two they moved from the hotel into the yacht, so that Leanda could get used to life aboard ship while conditions were still comfortable, and any gaps in their arrangements could be detected in time. Up to the very last moment there were things to

51

do, and things to buy. Conway came back from his final round of purchases with a large brown paper parcel—a gift, he said, for Leanda. She opened it wonderingly—and out fell a mat, with the word "Welcome" on it. "For your hero!" Conway said.

On the last day they saw the emigration people and the customs and got clearance for the Seychelles without difficulty. Afterward there was final business to do with Ionides. He brought greetings and good wishes from Metaxas, received that day by code, and the news that a further thousand pounds had been paid into Conway's account. The two men completed some rather technical financial arrangements, devised by Metaxas, which would seem to show that Ionides had made a genuine sale of *Thalia* to Conway, and at a good profit, if anyone should ever get around to questioning him. They also rehearsed once more the plans for Kastella at Malindi. Then, with a surprisingly emotional little speech about the importance of the enterprise, Ionides wished them a safe passage, and left them. In the evening, several Yacht Club members dropped in to say goodby, and stayed for drinks. But by eleven peace had descended on the creek. Conway spent a little time with his charts and the *Indian Ocean Pilot*, while Leanda cleared up. Then they turned in.

At dawn, they sailed.

2

As soon as they were clear of the harbor, Conway streamed the patent log and set *Thalia* on her course. Heureuse lay due east, in almost the same latitude as Mombasa, but with the wind heading the ship from the southeast and likely to go on doing so, the best he could steer without starving her was eighty-five degrees. Leeway on the long beat would carry her still further to the north, but one tack toward the end of the trip would put that right. At present the southeaster was a gentle sailing breeze, about force three, just sufficient to keep *Thalia's* sails asleep and pulling steadily at around four knots. The surface of the indigo sea was ruffled, but there were no white horses. The motion of the ship in the long swell was regular and easy.

Conway was fully occupied for a while, satisfying himself that all was well, trimming the sails to suit the wind and the ship, noting the angle of the wake to estimate the leeway. Then, around eight, he gave the tiller to Leanda. She was still very much of a tyro, but the breeze was steady and all she had to do

53

was keep an eye on the compass and steer the right course. Conway watched her for a moment, then gave her an encouraging nod and went below to prepare breakfast of cereal, eggs and coffee. His appetite was always good at sea and he liked his meals substantial. When the food was ready he called Leanda to eat and took the tiller himself. Then he breakfasted while she steered. The tests in Mombasa harbor had shown, as he'd expected, that *Thalia* wouldn't sail herself satisfactorily to windward, so while present conditions lasted they would always have to eat separately.

Afterward, Conway washed up and made all shipshape in the saloon and then went to sit beside Leanda in the cockpit. He had stripped to his shorts, for the morning was hot and on this tack the mainsail gave no shade. His back and shoulders were already tanned a deep walnut. Leanda, in loose white shirt and briefs, and with a bright yellow head scarf for protection, looked cool and faintly piratical. Conway glanced up at the sail as he came on deck, an instinctive action, and then around the horizon. The low-lying Kenya coast was no longer visible; there was nothing to be seen in any direction but water and sky. Probably there wouldn't be anything now until they neared Heureuse, for this was one of the loneliest oceans in the world, right off the shipping lanes. Their only companions were a few gulls, hovering above the stern, and the flying fish that shot from the sea like silver arrows, their delicate wings outstretched. Singly and in clouds they rose and dipped around the ship. Leanda watched entranced, till Conway pointed to the wandering compass needle and asked her where she thought she was going.

At noon he took his first sight, more to familiarize Leanda with the drill than because he needed to know their position so early. He had done it a thousand times on his own, but it would be less awkward with two. To Leanda, the operation looked most complicated. While she concentrated on steering a steady course, Conway braced himself against the main hatch, focusing the sextant telescope on the horizon. Then he moved the index bar to bring the reflected image of the sun close to the water, turned the screw for fine adjustment—and called, "Now!" At the signal, Leanda started the stop watch she was holding. They went through the drill three times, and then Conway went below to make his simple calculations. The third reading gave them a position only a few miles different from dead reckoning. In six hours they had covered nearly twenty-five nautical miles.

"Is that good?" Leanda asked.

"It could be a lot worse," Conway told her. "I've sometimes sailed all day and finished up further back than when I started!" He made the first penciled cross on the track chart, and the first entry in the log.

Leanda prepared the lunch and Conway cleared away, and at two in the afternoon they started their regular watchkeeping— four hours on and four off during the day, which would give them time for sleeping, and two-hour stints during the night. Leanda had insisted that there should be no "weaker vessel" stuff while conditions were easy, and Conway was ready enough to agree. But actually, on this first day, he was around all the time, busying himself with little jobs but keeping an eye on her.

So far he had scarcely had to touch the sheets. The wind remained true and steady. A few clouds gathered toward evening but there was no sign of any appreciable change in the weather. As the sun plunged into the sea, leaving a glorious sky behind it, Leanda said, "This is a very gentle baptism for me, isn't it?"

Conway smiled and nodded.

"Rather different," she said, "from that dreadful picture of sailing you drew for me at St.-Jean-de-Luz."

"It's a chance for you to get your sea legs," he told her. "The thing is, the southeast trades are about the most reliable winds in the world, but we're at the extreme northern edge of them here and at this season of the year they're moving south. They should carry us to Heureuse, with luck, but on the way back we'll be in the doldrum belt, and that's a very different kettle of fish. There'll be storms and calms—both pretty unpleasant."

"Oh, well," Leanda said, "sufficient unto the day. It's heavenly now."

As the quick tropical darkness fell, Conway lit the navigation lamps and the cabin lamps, and took a last look round the deck. Then, in the snug saloon, Leanda made up the bunks and prepared a light supper and they ate their separate meals.

There was a sharp warm shower around eleven, when Conway was at the helm, but it soon passed. At midnight Leanda took over again, slightly apprehensive in the empty darkness but determined not to show it. The ship, with its slight heel and its hissing wake, gave an illusion of speed, of rushing furiously through the night, and she kept a sharper lookout than was necessary. But the nervousness soon passed. The luminous compass card glowed comfortingly, the navigation lights threw cheerful pools of red and green on the heaving water. Conway, resting in the dim saloon, appeared to have full confidence in her. She certainly had confidence in him. He looked as cheerful and relaxed, out here on the ocean, as anyone she had ever seen.

Conway, in his bunk, knew from the sound and motion of the ship that all was well, but he watched Leanda through most of her two hours. Without raising his head he could just see her face—small, intense, concentrated, in the compass glow. He found it a companionable sight.

When he relieved her at two, he took a mug of tea out for her. "Anything to report?" he said, with a glance at the sail.

"Not a thing."

"How did you like your first night watch?"

"It was all right," she said. She suppressed a yawn. "It seemed rather a long time."

He laughed. "I once sat at *Tara's* tiller for twenty-eight consecutive hours, in a storm."

"I don't believe it!"

"It's true. I was so tired at the end I was breathing from memory! Okay, you'd better get a cat nap—four o'clock will be round in no time."

In a day or two they had settled into a regular, though by no means wearisome, routine. Leanda did the domestic chores and most of the cooking—which she soon found was one of the toughest jobs aboard. The first time she tried to fry anything, a sudden lurch of the ship sent the pan of hot fat flying across the saloon, burning her arm slightly and making a terrible mess. Apart from the hazards, she never quite got used to the smell of cooking in the confined space. But she pretended that she found it a pleasant change from being a secretary-conspirator,

57

and Conway believed her. She produced nothing fancy, which suited him well. Her one real experiment was when she cooked, at his suggestion, some of the flying fish that crashed against the sail every night and were found in the morning on the scale-slippery deck. According to Conway, flying fish were a delicacy, but those she served up were dry and full of bones, and she didn't try again. Apart from cooking, she swabbed down the decks every day, heaving buckets of crystal water up over the starboard rail with a strength that seemed out of proportion to her size. She also attended to the simple but repetitive job of filtering the day's supply of sea water through the rubber bags of the patent device and adding the little cubes of chemicals that made it drinkable. At first she had been a bit doubtful about using sea water for drinking, but after the first day she had to admit that it tasted as good as anything from a tap and that the advantages of having an unlimited supply without the need for storage were overwhelming. In between, when she wasn't cooking or filtering or swabbing, there was steering to be done, and clothes to wash, and the ravages of sun and salt to be made good. One way and another, she never seemed to have a moment to spare. Conway found her extremely efficient, philosophical over minor hardships, and tactfully self-effacing when he was busy.

Getting enough sleep was her main problem. She had not yet learned to drop off at will, as Conway always did, and she found the watchkeeping disturbing. She could have slept perfectly at the tiller, where the compass card had a mesmeric effect on her, particularly at night, but the thought of Conway rushing out to see why the sails were flapping was too awful to contemplate. The saloon was hot in the daytime, in spite of its ventilators, and scarcely bearable when some of them had to be shut to keep out flying spray. Shafts of sunlight were a nuisance, and at night the noise of the water on the other side of the planking tended to keep her awake. So, occasionally, did the thought that there was only an inch of wood between her and the ocean, and that where they were it was about three miles deep! But gradually she got used to the conditions, as by now she was completely used to the motion of the ship, and in the end she slept adequately.

Conway was busy most of the time. There were the regular daily jobs—taking the log reading, checking the chronometer with the radio time signal, taking sights from the sun at noon or, if necessary, from the stars at dusk or dawn, marking up the chart, writing up the log. There were the occasional jobs— filling the lamps and stove, giving a touch of grease to the blocks, cleaning the chromium fittings, running the engine for a while to keep it in shape, checking the stores. For short periods, when it wasn't his watch, he would lie and read, or listen briefly to the radio news before switching off to save the battery. But mostly, when he wasn't sleeping or working, he was on deck with Leanda.

Occasionally, some unusual incident would break the routine. Leanda, in her off time, liked to go forward to the bows and lean out over the pulpit to watch the ship's stem cleaving the sea— "an attractive but overdressed figurehead," Conway called her. From there she sighted one day a spouting whale, which came unpleasantly close to *Thalia* before it finally disappeared. Once, too, an unusually large shark came right alongside, turning on

59

its back so that its vicious teeth were clearly visible and then scraping its belly against the keel of the ship. It stayed around so long that Conway went to get the shotgun from the forecabin to drive it away, but he'd scarcely reappeared when it sheered off and they didn't see it again. There were other, and pleasanter, creatures to watch—schools of playful porpoises gamboling along in the wake of the ship, and blue-and-black-striped pilot fish that kept to the shady side when there was one, and blue and silver bonitos. Once or twice Conway did a little fishing with a hand line, but the fish began to lose their dazzling tropical colors as soon as they were brought on deck and Leanda said she preferred to watch them in the water.

Most of the time, nothing happened at all. They seemed to be sailing through an endless desert of sea, featureless, unchanging, and awe-inspiring in its absolute emptiness. As one similar day followed another, with nothing around them but the same heaving blue waste, it was only the marks on the track chart that convinced Leanda they were getting anywhere at all. One morning, as Conway came up from the saloon with "coffee for all hands," she suddenly said, "You know, Mike, there might be no one else on this planet except us two!"

"It's not a bad thought," he said, with a grin.

She ignored that. "It's so hard to keep anything in perspective. The world seems so remote. I have to keep on reminding myself that we still belong, that we're actually on a terribly important mission, that there's a man called Kastella on an island somewhere out there, and that we're on our way to rescue him. It doesn't seem real."

"That's how you get at sea," Conway said.

"But I *want* it to be real."

"If we kept on sailing for a month or two you probably wouldn't care any more. You'd get the cosmic view."

"Like you?"

"That's right. Human antics seem pretty trivial in the middle of an ocean."

"Including the antic of trying to earn twenty thousand pounds?" Leanda said. "I'd say that was pretty small beer against the background of the universe. You're not very consistent."

Conway said, "Let's change the subject! How's the coffee?"

They continued to run down the latitude, and by the end of the first week they had made good nearly four hundred and eighty miles. They had had one excellent day's run of ninety miles, when the wind had freshened, still from the same quarter, and they had enjoyed an exhilarating beat through a choppy sea with salt spray flying over the bows and the mainsail hard as a drum. They had had one poor day of thirty-five miles, when the trade wind had seemed to be dying away altogether. But the average had been high, partly because of an east-going current which, in good winds and poor, carried them steadily toward their objective.

Leanda, by now, was shaping up into quite a promising sailor. She no longer pointed the ship so close to the wind that it lost way and wallowed sluggishly, or pulled in the jib sheet when Conway told her to haul in the main. She watched everything that he did, and, when she didn't understand why, she asked. He responded to her interest, explaining and demonstrating with the patience of a devotee. They got on excellently together. After a week of close companionship they were both more friendly and more personally interested in each other.

One evening, when Leanda was steering and Conway was sitting opposite her in the cockpit, whipping a piece of codline, he suddenly said, "You know, I'm glad I brought you."

Leanda said, "Because I can cook, I suppose!"

'No—but you're a nice person to have around. I've kind of got used to you."

"You'll look well if I've spoiled you for sailing alone," she said. "It'll certainly be very different."

Leanda gazed around the empty sea. "I simply don't know how you can bear it on your own. Nothing to look at, week after week, except water! It's not my idea of seeing the world."

Conway grinned. "Wasn't it John Stuart Mill who said that the best way to see the world was to get away from it?"

"Was it? You're always quoting funny little tags."

"Pearls of wisdom, accumulated at *Tara's* tiller!"

"Well, I still think it's an extraordinary way to live."

"For that matter," Conway said, "I find your way of living pretty extraordinary—sneaking about with leaflets, rioting in the streets, being sent to jail, organizing political propaganda . . . You can't say it's natural. Most girls of your age would be thinking of getting married and raising a family."

"I've plenty of time for that," Leanda said. "I'm only political about Spyros, you know. Once it's free, I shall turn to other things. I'll be glad to. . . . But you—what happens to you in the end? Are you going to be an Ancient Mariner?"

"I might be. . . . Old Joshua Slocum never got tired of it."

"Who was he?"

"He was a man who sailed round the world on his own—till he disappeared. He was supposed to have been run down in the dark."

"What a dismal prospect!" Leanda said.

"Oh, well, maybe I'll get fed up with it in the end. . . . Perhaps I'll be like the sea captain who retired."

"What sea captain?"

"He'd spent forty years afloat. One day he put an oar over his shoulder and walked straight inland. He walked and walked, until one morning, after many weeks, a boy stopped him in the street and said, 'Hi, mister, what's that thing over your shoulder?' Then the sea captain knew he'd reached a place where he could spend the rest of his days in peace!"

Leanda smiled. "It's a nice story. . . . Perhaps you'll go back to Ireland in the end. People say it's lovely."

"It is indeed," Conway said. "Pretty as a picture . . . I remember a place my father and mother used to take me to for picnics sometimes—the wild pansies grew so thick on the dunes you could scarcely move for them, and the fuchsia flowers in the hedges were as big as plums."

"What did your father do, Mike?"

"Oh, he did a lot of things, but toward the end he was keeping a small hotel, a holiday place, up in the wilds of Donegal. He was very sentimental about Ireland. I can see him now, sitting in the bar with a bunch of his friends, singing passionate songs about Ireland's struggle in a voice choking with sobs. He was a lovely man, though—a big, tough man with a soft heart. He'd have liked me to take over the place, the way fathers do,

63

but I was tired of the bogs and wanted to get away on my own. So he paid for me to go to Dublin, to the university, and I became an engineer."

"And then what?"

"Then I went to Canada—Montreal, Quebec, all sorts of places. That's a fine country, Canada. I was there quite a while, helping to build bridges and dams and things. The trouble was I couldn't keep still—I'm a real maverick. I started sailing, first on the lakes and then on the sea, and I got mad about boats, and in the end I just packed up and sailed away and I've been sailing ever since."

"Are your parents still alive?"

"No, they both died while I was in Canada—rest their souls. . . ." He was silent for a while. "Maybe I *will* go back to Ireland someday—just for old times' sake. I'd like to smell the peat again. I'd like to sail into Donegal Bay, to Killybegs, in my own ship—perhaps this ship, who knows?" He looked at Leanda and grinned. "Let's hope they're not keeping Kastella on a chain!"

By the end of the tenth day, *Thalia* had been blown so far to the north that a change of course was essential if they weren't to miss Heureuse by fifty miles. Leanda, whose eagerness to reach the island and get on with the rescue operation was growing steadily now they were so near, suggested they should use the engine and motor straight there. But Conway was against that. Later on, he said, they might have to rely on the engine a good deal, and as it wasn't at all certain they'd be able to get the right sort of Diesel fuel in Heureuse they'd better husband what they'd got. Next morning early, therefore, he put *Thalia* about, and they started a long board on a course a little west of south. The wind had fallen light, and they had to keep going all day and all night and part of the next day before Conway was satisfied that they would make Heureuse on one more tack. Then, with the island well over the lee bow, he turned the ship again onto the eighty-five-degree course.

There was a little excitement next morning when Conway, at the tiller, suddenly called "Sail ho!" and Leanda came rushing up from the saloon to see a three-masted schooner bearing down on them from the north. She looked a fine sight from a distance, but as she drew abreast they saw that her hull was rusted and her dirty old sails patched like a quilt. Conway thought she was probably trading between the Seychelles and Mauritius. She was soon hull down, and for the rest of the day *Thalia* had the sea to herself again.

That evening Conway began studying his arrival charts. Heureuse was the largest of a group of islands and islets that rose from a shallow plateau. The plateau itself covered many hundreds of square miles, and on the west extended more than fifty miles from Heureuse. The long, deep-water crossing was almost over; soon, *Thalia* would have only a fathom or two under her—and the dangers of coral were very fresh in Conway's mind. But on the west, he was relieved to see, there appeared to be a broad, unobstructed approach through the cays and islands. Provided the chart showed all the hazards, there should be no serious difficulty.

It was Leanda who, on the fourteenth day, suddenly announced that she could see a tree growing out of the ocean. It was the top of a coconut palm, rising from some invisible spit of sand perhaps ten miles away on the starboard bow. Soon, other trees appeared, singly and in clumps. There were islands now on both sides—most of them, according to the chart, uninhabited cays, but some with little copra-trading stations and a scattering of huts. Birds had suddenly appeared—clouds of terns that fluttered over green shallows where a rippling tide race stirred the water. There was an exciting tang of wood smoke in the air. In the late afternoon another human contact was made—a solitary boatman paddling a double-ended pirogue, apparently quite unworried by the ocean swell.

Conway took special care with his sights that evening, getting a perfect fix from three stars just before darkness blotted out the horizon. They had now only about thirty-five miles to go, but these would be the most hazardous miles of all. There was no question of alternate watches any more. Conway took the tiller, his ears alert for the warning sound of surf. Leanda, beside him, watched for any fleck of white. But they heard nothing, and saw nothing, and sailed peacefully on.

It was a heavenly night, warm as a caress. The stars were brilliant. Over the tip of the boom, to the north, the Plow swung gently, upside down. Away to the south, the Southern Cross blazed. The air was sweet with the scents from the land.

Conway looked down at Leanda. "Well," he said, "only a few hours more. I must say I feel quite sorry."

"It's been a good trip," Leanda said.

"It's been a very short trip. I don't feel ready for the land yet."

"We've a job to do," Leanda reminded him. "We're not just out for a sail."

"I can't think of jobs tonight," Conway said. He gazed up at the starlit canopy of the sky. "Lovely, isn't it? 'The great out-of-doors . . .'"

"Beautiful."

"What was it Stevenson said? —'To live out of doors . . .'" Abruptly, he broke off.

" 'To live out of doors'—what?" Leanda asked.

"It's odd," Conway said, "but I can't remember the rest of the quotation. . . . Look, if we've got to keep awake all night, why don't we have some coffee?"

It was a splendid and exciting dawn. Against a flushed sky, Heureuse stood out boldly, straight ahead and very close. It looked big and solid, a considerable chunk of land. Unlike the other islands they had seen, it rose impressively to a granite knob so high that the top was wreathed in cloud. Coconut palms climbed far up the hillside from the empty beaches. Trees covered the upper slopes, too. Everything looked lush and green and inviting.

Leanda, studying the shore through the binoculars, said softly, "I wonder where we shall find him."

Conway grunted, and bent over his chart. The island, fifteen miles long by about ten at its widest part, was shaped like a pear, and it was the pointed end they were approaching. The capital, Port Edward, lay on the other side of the point, a mile or so up the coast. As they closed the land, the high ground took their wind and *Thalia's* sails drooped. Conway started the engine and they motored round the promontory over a glassy sea. There was a tall white lighthouse marking the end of the harbor channel. As soon as they were in plain view of the port, Conway let the anchor go in four fathoms and hoisted the yellow "Q" flag—"My vessel is healthy and I request free pratique." Leanda prepared breakfast while he wound in the log line and scraped it clean of the sea creatures, large as olives, that had somehow managed to get a grip on it even though it had been spinning all the while. Then, for the first time since Mombasa, they ate a meal together, a cheerful celebration. They were just clearing away when a launch came out with the port doctor aboard, a young colored man who welcomed them warmly and quickly gave them permission to enter the port. They followed the launch in, steering between fierce-looking submarine cliffs of coral that made them glad of the pilotage, and tied up at the quieter end of the quay under directions from the harbor master. In a few minutes, customs and immigration formalities were completed. They had arrived!

Their sudden appearance caused quite a stir on the jetty. A line of creoles, jogging between a shed and a small coastal schooner with headloads of green bananas, stopped short as though someone had switched off a conveyor belt. A man unloading a large turtle kept it dangling by its flippers while he exchanged excited comment with his neighbors in an unintelligible French patois. Children raced up noisily to inspect the new arrival, and strapping Negresses broke into shrill, hysterical giggles. Conway and Leanda stayed below for a while, tidying up the ship, and gradually the interest subsided. Then Conway went off to get water from the hydrant on the quay, lots of water, and they took turns having their most enjoyable bath since Africa. Conway changed into clean shorts and shirt, and Leanda put on an attractive cotton frock and spent a long time making up her face.

"Are we going to live on board while we're here?" she asked, when she emerged into the cockpit at last.

Conway nodded. "I'll feel safer if we do—we don't want to take any chances with *Thalia*. Besides, it'll give us much more freedom of action."

"That's true. . . . Well, now, what's our plan?"

"This is *my* plan," Conway said. He bent and kissed her lightly on the mouth. "Darling Leanda, you look beautiful!"

She stared at him. "What's that for?"

"Now that we're here we've got to start being affectionate again. The eyes of the enemy are upon us!"

"I see . . . All right, within reason . . ."

"We've also got to look as much like tourists as possible. Better get your camera and sunglasses."

She went below and fetched them. "What are we going to *do*, though?" she said, as she reappeared. "Where do we start?"

"Well, we mustn't start by showing too much interest in Kastella, that's obvious."

"We mustn't show too little, either. Anyone coming here would be sure to know about him, and ask questions."

"All the same, I'd prefer to wait until the subject crops up naturally."

"Who will it crop up with?"

Conway grinned. "The governor, I hope."

"The governor!"

"That's right. I'm not very well up in these things, being Irish, but I've always understood the correct drill on arriving in a British colony is to call and pay one's respects. Anyway, I'll ring up Government House and see what happens."

"You mean now?"

"Well, we'll wait a bit—we don't want to give the impression we've rushed straight from the boat to a phone box. Let's go and have a look round the town."

He tucked her hand in his and guided her along the uneven quay. To both of them, the ground seemed to sway a little after their two weeks in *Thalia*. As they passed the harbor master's office, Conway looked in and arranged for someone to keep an eye on the boat. Then they walked on into Port Edward.

Their first impression was of a busy, lively, colorful town with a lot of character. On the far side of the harbor, more schooners and ketches were loading and unloading a variety of exotic cargoes. Shiny cars raced past an incongruous-looking "Major Road Ahead" sign with blaring horns. Crowds of cheerful, amiable people, ranging in color from jet black to white, but most of them African in origin, thronged the streets and shops, filling the air with their high-pitched chatter and sudden squeals of laughter. There were women with flat shiny noses and enormous buttocks carrying woolly-capped babies strapped to their backs; men with black skins and Western features; young girls with high-heeled shoes and elegant handbags and drifts of white powder over their chocolate complexions; elderly empire build-

70

ers in white shorts and stockings and sun helmets; European wives paying calls; old Negresses in black skirts, with cloths knotted round their heads; and young Negroes wearing straw hats of which little but the crown was left. There was no lack of subjects to photograph.

The hub of the place seemed to be a large square, surrounded by two-story public buildings and trading company offices of wood and concrete, and dominated by a cathedral with a huge belfry and a façade of staggering ugliness. At one end of the square there was a taxi-and-rickshaw rank, and a statue of Edward VII on a black plinth; at the other, a large dragon tree, giving shade to a score of young Negroes in white shirts and trousers who were lolling, sleeping, playing mouth organs and strumming guitars, or just vacantly staring. There was a faint stir as Leanda stopped to photograph a small boy who was carrying a letter on his head with a large stone on top to keep it down, and a dozen pairs of ruminating eyes remained on her till she was out of sight. Conway suggested they should have a look at the market, but it smelled powerfully of dried fish and rancid coconut oil and they soon passed on. Moving slowly in the languorous heat, they made their way along untidy streets lined with crazy shacks that seemed to be built entirely of corrugated iron and flattened petrol cans. Away from the center, most of the town seemed to be like that. Port Edward wasn't, they agreed, much of a place after all.

Back in the square, they turned into a bar and quenched their thirst with two lime squashes. Conway bought an English-language paper, the Port Edward *Star*, from a passing newsboy, and left Leanda to look for any references to Kastella while he went off to telephone Government House.

He was back in about five minutes. "Well, that's that," he said. "His Excellency will be happy to see us at half past three this afternoon!"

"Oh, good! Who did you talk to?"

"His A.D.C.—a naval commander named Fletcher . . . Have you found anything about Kastella?"

"Not a word. For all the interest this paper takes, he might not be on the island at all."

"Perhaps he isn't," Conway said solemnly. "Perhaps they've moved him somewhere else."

"You're not serious!" Leanda looked really worried.

Conway smiled. "You do rise, don't you? No, I think he's here, all right—it's just that he isn't news after all this time. . . . Now let's see if we can find somewhere bearable for lunch."

Government House, they learned, lay some distance out of the town, so at three o'clock they hired a taxi to take them there. The road soon began to climb out of the urban huddle, but the slummy aspect of the view remained. Since there was little level ground to build on, the shacks were now perched precariously on piles of stone and on timber stilts. With their untidy coconut thatch and ramshackle walls and patches of rusty iron, they looked to Conway more like something that Huck Finn and Tom Sawyer might have run up for fun as a weekend camp. On the beaten ground around them, black babies with bare bottoms groveled in the dust, and scraggy dogs and chickens picked and foraged in the garbage. Tall mangoes and breadfruit trees, bananas and bamboos, shaded, but scarcely cloaked, the squalor.

A faint smell of open drains hung over the hillside. They passed an old man smoking a pipe on a doorstep, who scarcely raised his eyes, and some young women pounding clothes on a rock, and a modest young man soaping himself over his shorts at a standpipe. Then the huts thinned out and there was a stretch of unspoiled country with rock-strewn gulleys and trickling streams and lush ferns. Presently more houses appeared—neat houses, with verandas, on concrete bases; and modern bungalows like Ionides' home in Mombasa, with fences and gates and garages and an air of prosperity. In a few moments they were entering the grounds of the governor's residence—a long, white, attractive building, with a veranda supported on columns, and a garden with flowering shrubs and a terrace, and lawns of close-cut grass that looked green and pleasant to their sea-accustomed eyes. Someone, they saw, had been playing croquet. . . .

They had barely given their names to the white-coated servant when a handsome, burly man advanced across the hall with outstretched hand. "Hullo," he said cordially, "glad you were able to come. I'm Fletcher. . . . Come on in. H. E.'s looking forward to meeting you."

They preceded him into a large, light room with statuary in the corners and portraits of the Queen and Winston Churchill on opposite walls. A slim, graying man of sixty or so, in shorts and a bush shirt, rose from a desk to greet them. Fletcher said, "Mr. and Mrs. Michael Cornford . . . Sir George Hollis."

"Well, this is a very pleasant surprise," the governor said, as they sat down. "We don't see many new faces here except when the mail steamers arrive, and heaven knows that isn't very often. I hear you've sailed from Africa in your own yacht?"

Conway nodded. "We were actually making for the Seychelles but we ran short of fresh food so we decided to put in here for supplies."

"Yes, I see. . . . I'm sorry my wife isn't here. She has a hospital committee this afternoon, but she'll certainly want to meet you. . . . How long do you expect to stay?"

"Oh, perhaps a week or two," Conway said. "We're hoping to make a round trip—on to the Seychelles and back via Mauritius —but we're not pressed for time."

"A holiday trip, eh?" Hollis was looking at Leanda with interest and appreciation.

Leanda smiled. "We're refugees from the English winter, Sir George."

"Very nice, too, Mrs. Cornford—and most enterprising. How would you like to do that trip, Fletcher?"

"Not me," the commander said. "Never could stand the sea! I like my comforts."

"Well, they neither of them look as though they've come to any harm," Hollis said. "How big is your yacht, Cornford?"

"About eight tons," Conway told him.

"My word, she is small, isn't she . . . ? Did you have a good passage?"

"It couldn't have been better—we came across like a train."

"H'm—well, this is quite an occasion. I'd like to have a look at your ship sometime. I do a little sailing myself, when I can get away from these beastly papers."

Conway said, "We'd be very happy to see you aboard, sir— wouldn't we, darling?"

Leanda smiled. "Of course."

74

"Where's she tied up?" Fletcher asked. "At the jetty?"

"Yes, right at the end."

"Well, I don't want to frighten you, but you'll probably find her full of cockroaches when you get back!"

"We're not very easily frightened," Leanda said.

"That I can believe," Hollis said. He glanced across at Fletcher. "Well, I hope you'll have an enjoyable stay here. It's a very lovely island and full of historical interest—there's even a genuine eighteenth-century pirates' lair, if you like that sort of thing. There's a splendid view from the peak, too, if you can get someone to take you up.... Grant's the man for that, isn't he, Fletcher? He'll be along here tonight.... Look, I wonder if you'd care to dine with us this evening?"

"It's very kind of you," Leanda said. "We'd love to."

Hollis nodded. "We usually dress, but . . ." he smiled at Conway, "it doesn't really matter if the sea chest won't run to it."

"Oh, I dare say we can rustle up something," Conway said.

"Good. Then we'll expect you at seven-thirty. My wife will be delighted.... How are you getting back, by the way?"

"We've a taxi outside."

"That's the idea—you never want to get separated from your transport in this climate. But don't bother about a taxi tonight—I'll send my car for you."

"That's extremely good of you," Conway said. "Good-by, then, sir, till this evening...." Leanda smiled, and Fletcher shepherded them out.

In the taxi, Conway said, "Well, they managed that very smoothly, didn't they? First they have us up to give us the once-over and make sure our fingernails are clean. Then they ask us to dinner. Very English!"

"I thought Sir George was sweet," Leanda said. "I really hated being such a fraud."

Conway grinned. "Watch yourself! You have nice instincts. Don't let them get the better of you."

"You needn't worry," Leanda said. "I won't."

They were just about changed and ready when the governor's car rolled up to the quay at a quarter past seven that evening. Conway's white jacket was a bit creased but his black tie was impeccable, and Leanda looked charming in a frock of palest yellow organza. Fifteen minutes later they were being shown into Lady Hollis' drawing room, where the rest of the guests were already assembled and cocktails were being served. The restrained buzz of conversation died away as Lady Hollis, gray-haired and gracious, welcomed the new arrivals and introduced them. Conway, mindful of the need for useful contacts, made a special note of all the names and faces. There was an old gentleman named Rankin, pink and cherubic and mild-mannered, who turned out to be a peer. There was also Lady Rankin. There was a dark, broad-shouldered man who was introduced as Colonel Baker and who turned out, rather disconcertingly, to be the island's commissioner of police. He, too, had his wife with him. There was a woman named Peabody, wife of a professor whose absence from the party was not accounted for; Grant, a shipping man, whose services in climbing "the Peak" had been offered by the governor, and *his* wife; and a shy young man named Carruthers, who was apparently engaged in some kind of local fishery research.

76

FOR LEANDA

Conway was buttonholed at once by Mrs. Peabody, who said she was sure he must have had a most *adventurous* voyage across the ocean and proceeded to describe at great length the rough crossing that she and her husband had experienced in the liner that had brought them to Heureuse six weeks before. He was rescued by Mrs. Grant, a plummy contralto, who asked him if he had seen many sharks and drew the young fisheries man into the conversation, while the police commissioner stood by with his head slightly on one side, listening. After a few moments the A.D.C. took Conway off to show him the table arrangements, which were pinned up on a board, and break the news to him that he would be taking Mrs. Peabody in to dinner. Soon afterward, dinner was served, and Conway gave the lady his arm and they all trooped into the dining room as though it were an ark.

Mrs. Peabody, who was dressed over all in flowered pink silk, turned out to be even more garrulous than Conway had feared. Her husband, it seemed, was an expert on the processing of seaweed and she evidently shared his interest for she talked unceasingly about it. When Conway ventured to interpose a comment, her attention immediately wandered. In the end, he contented himself with nodding, and let his own attention wander. Leanda, he saw, was getting on extremely well with Colonel Baker on the other side of the table, but Mrs. Baker was wilting a little under Lord Rankin's smooth flow. Rankin, according to the A.D.C., had been an éminence grise in the Cabinet Secretariat before World War II and was now collecting material for a book on colonial development. His immediate interest, however, seemed to be much nearer home, for he was talking about his stomach. With the ear that wasn't taking in facts about the iodine content of seaweed, Conway could hear him totting up the calorie value of each dish as it was served and comparing it with that of the patent cereals that he and his wife had brought out from England in order to maintain a proper dietetic balance.

Conway switched his free ear to the end of the table. Dietetics had got a grip there, too. Grant was saying that the local breadfruit was a very poor substitute for the potato, and that it had really been the ruin of the island, since a Negro had only to have a single breadfruit tree in his garden to decide that he need do no work at all. Lady Hollis raised her voice a little and asked Conway how they managed about meals aboard *Thalia,* and for a few minutes the conversation became general while he and Leanda talked of their ocean crossing. But sailing reminded someone of a bad storm the previous year, and storms of a tennis party that had been washed out at the club last week, and at that point Lady Hollis got up and the ladies withdrew and Conway was encouraged to talk on alone as the port circulated.

The topic flagged at last, and there was a lull while the glasses were refilled. Then Grant suddenly said, "How's the emperor, Colonel?"

"Oh, fussy as ever," Baker said.

The governor smiled at Conway. "Our distinguished prisoner, Cornford—Alexander Kastella."

"Ah, yes, of course," Conway said. "I was going to ask you about him. . . . So that's what you call him—the emperor?"

"The title seemed to fit," Hollis said. "An island prisoner—and the man does seem to suffer from a mild form of *folie de grandeur.*"

"The poor man's Bonaparte," Grant said. "Sees himself as an eventual dictator, if you ask me. Nothing he likes better than ordering people about. . . . How many servants has he got now, Colonel?"

"Eight," the commissioner said.

"Fantastic! Why, he only needs a few horses and he'll be able to form his own Household Cavalry!"

Baker smiled. "We try to humor him as far as possible, Cornford—it makes life easier. But he still complains. It's deliberate, of course—he can't do us any vital damage at the moment but he can still harry us. . . . Did I tell you, H. E.?—he sent in a written protest yesterday about one of Franklin's 'boys' singing in the garden—said it disturbed his thoughts!"

"Extraordinary!" Hollis said.

"Where do you keep him?" Conway asked. "Is he locked up?"

"Good heavens, no," Baker said, "not in a place like this. . . . He has a bungalow over on the other side of the island—he's practically a free man. He gave his parole that he wouldn't go into the villages or talk to any of the black chaps except his own servants—we had to insist on that in case he tried to stir up agitation in the colony. But otherwise he does pretty much as he likes."

"How does he spend his time?"

"Oh, he swims a lot, reads, writes a good deal. . . ."

"He's working on a constitution for Spyros, ready for when it becomes independent," H. E. said with his gentle smile.

Grant snorted. "The Code Kastella!"

"He's a lawyer, you know," Baker said. "An able chap, and quite charming when he wants to be, but a born troublemaker."

79

"Do you suppose he'll be here very long?" Conway said.

Baker shrugged. "Who knows? He can't go soon enough for me, I can tell you that."

"Or me, Colonel," the governor said. "Well, shall we join the ladies?"

There was no further talk of Kastella. In the drawing room, chairs had been disposed in a casual-audience fashion, and a pale young man appeared and for half an hour played pieces from Chopin and Debussy on the pianoforte to polite applause. At nine-thirty, Hollis suggested that the men should help themselves to whisky. At ten, Lord Rankin said it was time he was getting to bed, and the party began to break up. As Conway and Leanda prepared to leave, the police commissioner and his wife closed in on them purposefully.

"Is there any chance you could lunch with us tomorrow, at the club?" Mrs. Baker said. "We'd so much like you to meet some of our friends."

Leanda smiled. "It would be very nice," she said. "Thank you."

"Are you living on your boat?"

"For the moment, yes."

"Then I'll pick you up there at a quarter to twelve. All right?"

"Lovely," Leanda said.

As soon as they were in the governor's car, with a plate-glass window between themselves and the driver, Conway said, "Well, did you learn anything interesting?"

Leanda shook her head. "Not a thing. They were talking about how expensive servants were, most of the time. What about you?"

"I picked up a thing or two," Conway said. He recounted in detail the conversation over the port. Leanda listened with horrified fascination.

"God," she said, "how smug and superior they sound!"

"They were, rather."

"I honestly don't think I could have sat through it—I'd have blown up."

"Then it's just as well you retired with the ladies!"

"What do they *expect* him to do while he's here—compose sonnets to them? Of course he gives trouble. Really, they're insufferable."

"This afternoon you thought the governor was charming!"

"Well, his attitude isn't. . . . *Folie de grandeur*, indeed! Imagine an Englishman saying that of anyone!" She was silent for a moment or two. Then she said, "Mike, we haven't got very far, have we?"

"Oh, I don't know—we've made a start. We know Kastella is reasonably free."

"We were pretty sure of that before."

"Well, we've made some useful contacts—and got ourselves another invitation."

"Yes, from the commissioner of police! He probably intends to keep an eye on us all the time."

"I shouldn't think so—he hasn't any reason to be suspicious. You made a hit with him, that's all. Actually, it may turn out to be rather a good thing—we could hardly start our inquiries under more respectable auspices."

81

"We haven't even discovered where Kastella is, yet. 'The other side of the island' is terribly vague."

"It's a pretty small island. Anyway, we can't hurry things."

"I wish I had your patience," Leanda said.

Mrs. Baker turned up at the quay sharp at a quarter to twelve next day. Leanda showed her over *Thalia*—which she thought most attractive but *so* tiny—and then they drove to the club, a long low wooden building situated half a mile out of town on a piece of ground carved out of a coconut grove overlooking the sea. Everything about it was as English as loving imitation could make it—the chintz-covered chairs, the racks of magazines, the small library smelling slightly of mildew, the billiard room, the photographs of successful ball-hitting teams on the walls, the sternly worded notices—"It has come to the attention of the committee . . . !"—and, of course, the bar. There was already a good deal of pre-lunch activity, with a fair cross-section of the island's wives, husbands and bachelors talking shop and cars, sport and gossip, with a few mild arguments and a great deal of loud laughter. Colonel Baker was waiting to greet his guests, and took them in for drinks. During the next half hour he introduced them to so many new people that even Conway lost track of the faces. Everyone seemed to have heard of their arrival, and everyone seemed delighted to meet them. Conway constantly had his diary out, making a note of invitations for drinks or lunch.

"It looks as though we'll have to stay longer than a fortnight!" Leanda said, during a brief lull.

"We shall all take a very poor view if you don't, Mrs. Cornford," the colonel told her gallantly. "No one ever comes here for less than two months—and after all, your time's your own, isn't it? You must join the club—you'll meet absolutely everyone here."

Leanda said, "Isn't there any color bar?"

Baker looked a bit startled. "Well, we don't actually have any colored chaps *in* the club, but I wouldn't call it a color bar—they wouldn't like it themselves. . . ."

Conway gave Leanda's ankle a sharp tap. She said, "No, I suppose not. . . ."

"Wouldn't feel comfortable, you know . . ." The colonel broke off as another couple came to the bar—a red-faced, hearty-looking man in riding breeches, and a very tall, handsome woman. "Ah, hullo, Tom! Morning, Wendy! You two haven't met Mr. and Mrs. Cornford, have you. . . ? Tom and Wendy Franklin."

There were more handshakes. Conway was trying to remember where he had heard the name Franklin. Suddenly he placed it. "You're not the Franklin whose 'boy' sings, are you?" he asked with a smile.

Franklin looked puzzled. "Whose boy sings. . . ?"

"We were hearing about a complaint that had been made—by Alexander Kastella. . . ."

Franklin gave a loud guffaw. "Oh, *that!* Yes, by jove—yes, I'm the chap. Confounded impudence!"

Baker said, "What are you having, Wendy—gin and French? Pink for you, Tom?"

"Thanks, old boy."

Conway said, "He's a neighbor of yours, then, is he?"

"Kastella? Yes, I can almost spit through his window—sometimes feel like it, too. Why they had to shove the blighter next to us I don't know."

"You know very well," Baker said. "We had to put him somewhere, and your end of the island's the emptiest. . . ." He explained to Conway. "Tom Franklin owns about half the coconuts in the colony—and, believe me, that's a lot of coconuts!"

"I'd trade them all for a nice yacht and a bit of free time to sail her," Franklin said. "I really envy you two. . . ! Where are you staying, by the way?"

"We're living in *Thalia*," Leanda said.

"What, down in the harbor?—that's a bit squalid, isn't it. . . ? I say, why don't you come and spend the weekend with us at La Pleasaunce—we'd love that, wouldn't we, Wendy? It's not a bad spot—quiet, you know, but jolly good swimming. I've got to come into town again on Saturday morning—I could pick you up. What do you say?"

Leanda looked at Conway, her eyes shining. "It sounds absolutely marvelous," she said. "We'd love to, wouldn't we, Mike?"

"We would indeed, darling," Conway said.

There were three days to go before the weekend—days which Conway and Leanda spent in an unproductive round of hard-drinking parties and active but irrelevant expeditions about the colony. It seemed wise to keep away from the Franklins' end of the island until the official visit, and no new facts emerged about Kastella. The weather was trying. The trade winds had finally died away, leaving Port Edward sweltering in a pool of calm. On the second day there was a shattering thunderstorm, with a deluge of rain from writhing pinnacles of cloud. The nights aboard *Thalia* were a stifling ordeal. A net that Conway had rigged over the door kept out mosquitoes and moths after dark, but other things managed to get in by day—Fletcher's cockroaches, and flying ants, and spiders of quite astonishing size, shape and celerity. Around the harbor, pariah dogs made such an uproar that it was difficult to sleep. Leanda chafed at the delay, and Conway grew liverish from his unaccustomed intake of alcohol. But at last, Saturday came, and shortly before noon they left in Franklin's Humber for La Pleasaunce, having first arranged for their trusty boatwatcher to sleep on *Thalia's* deck in their absence.

The Franklin estate was ten miles from Port Edward, on the southern side of the island. Apart from a shacky village or two which provided the estate labor, they encountered almost nothing on the way. As they approached their destination, the fierce, rocky contours they had become accustomed to on Heureuse gave place to a gently sloping coastal belt. The estate itself consisted almost entirely of coconut palms, stretching far inland from a broad scimitar of white beach. But round the house there was a magnificent garden, with trailing bougainvillaea and flame trees and hibiscus, and the largest gladioli Leanda had ever seen.

The bungalow, built of some attractive red wood, was set back in a clearing a hundred yards or so from the sea. It was large and square, with an unusual layout. There was one very big central dining-room-*cum*-sitting-room with double French doors at each end, which ran the whole length of the house. Opening out of this central room, on both sides were the bedrooms, offices and kitchen. They, in turn, opened onto a wooden veranda, screened against mosquitoes, which ran right round the house like the promenade deck of a ship.

The guests were given a pleasantly furnished, twin-bedded room on the north side. Conway left Leanda to do the unpacking and strolled out onto the veranda for a preliminary reconnaissance. From somewhere at the end of the house came sounds of singing, and high, cackling laughter. That, presumably, was the kitchen. To the right there was a storeroom; to the left, two more bedrooms, both unoccupied. The Franklins' own room must be on the other side of the house, which was probably just as well. Conway went on round to the front, where Tom Franklin had set out chairs in the shade of a big mango and was busy with a cocktail shaker.

"Well, this is certainly a delightful spot you've picked," Conway said, gazing around. "Swimming pool almost on your doorstep. Tennis court, too, I see . . . What's the wooden building through the trees?"

"That's the servants' annex," Franklin said. "We prefer not to have them in the house at night—they're a noisy lot."

"Aha! And the other one?" Conway motioned toward a white bungalow, just visible through the palms, a hundred yards or so away to the right.

"That!—oh, that's where the emperor lives."

Conway grinned. "It's a pretty long spit!"

"Not long enough, old boy. I don't know why they couldn't have sent him to the Seychelles—he could have had Makarios' old quarters there. But there's no accounting for these Whitehall wallahs."

"How is it there are two bungalows so close together?" Conway asked. "Were they both part of the same estate?"

"That's right," Franklin said. "I sold that one to a chap named Cornwallis-Smith, who wanted a weekend place, and then he died and it fell empty and it was still empty when Kastella was sent out here. H. E. thought it was just the place for him, and that was that."

"Does he really bother you much?"

"Kastella? No, not really—it's just that he can't help throwing his weight about, he's that sort of fellow, and occasionally we're the target because we're near."

"Do you ever talk to him?"

"No, there's a ban on that—H. E. won't allow any unofficial contacts. Not that I'd want to, anyway! Baker comes down and has a game of chess with him now and again, and of course he's got his sergeant to talk to."

"His bodyguard?"

"I suppose you could call Bates that, though there's no real supervision. Bates is more like an aide."

"It must be pretty lonely for the chap, all the same."

"I dare say it is. He often looks pretty glum, mooning up and down the beach."

"Doesn't he do any work? I thought H. E. said something about him working on a constitution."

"Oh, yes, he's doing that—he takes a deck chair down to the beach and sits there under a tree for hours, writing away. . . ." Franklin added ice to the mixture in the shaker. "By the way, how was your room? Think you'll be comfortable?"

"It feels like the Ritz after what we've been used to," Conway said.

"Good . . . I can hardly wait to hear all about your adventures. After lunch we must have a good old powwow."

Lunch—a perfectly served meal of avocado pear, turtle soup with sherry, and curried chicken—in fact had to be slept off, according to the custom of the house. Afterward, the four of them sat out under the tree and talked. Franklin was genuinely interested in *Thalia* and her voyage and plied Conway with questions. When that subject was exhausted Conway asked him about coconuts, and Franklin took him off to show him a bit of the estate and give him a short course on the running of the copra industry. Tea followed, and then more drinks, and some characteristic island talk over dinner about the laziness, dishonesty and immorality of the native population, and how it was a great mistake to educate them because then they all wanted to become clerks instead of working in the plantations.

It wasn't until they were alone together that night that Conway had a chance to tell Leanda the news he had gleaned about Kastella during the day. She looked worried.

"We've had a lot of luck getting here," she said, "but what happens now? How on earth are we going to contact him?"

"Frankly," Conway said, "I don't know."

"Have you any idea where he sleeps?"

"Not a clue. I asked all the questions I dared—I didn't want to seem too curious."

"Couldn't you slip out after dark and do a bit of investigating?"

"I could slip out, all right, and I might be able to find out where he sleeps—but I don't see how I could contact him safely. It's bound to be a bit of a shock for him, our turning up—he might easily give the show away before he realized what it was all about. Anyway, with all those servants and a police sergeant sleeping in the same bungalow—and perhaps a dog around . . ." Conway shook his head doubtfully.

"Well, we've got to do something, Mike, now we're here. This could be our only chance."

"It's no good doing anything rash," Conway said. "One false step, and Baker will have our passports checked—and that will be that. . . . Look, if Kastella moons about the beach as much as Franklin says he does, perhaps we'll have a chance to intercept him."

"But we're never left alone in the daytime—and the Franklins are such good hosts I don't suppose we will be. . . . Besides, we've only got tomorrow."

"We can always angle for another invitation," Conway said. "It's not going to help anyone if we get jailed."

"It's maddening! So near and yet so far!" Leanda gazed out over the starlit beach. "Everything's so quiet and still now. If only we could get one word to him, we could fix up a night meeting out there. The thing could be arranged in ten seconds."

"Well, we'll watch for a chance," Conway said. "We can't do more than that."

Next morning Franklin suggested they should all go out to the reef in his glass-bottomed boat and have a look at the coral. Conway, who had been hoping for an opportunity to inspect the lagoon at close quarters, declared it a splendid idea and quickly helped him haul the boat down the beach. It was a perfect day

89

for the trip. The water was milk-warm and smooth as silk, with only an occasional tiny wavelet curling lazily over at the very edge. The floor of the lagoon, Conway noticed, was sandy, with patches of short dark eel grass but no sign of any dangerous coral growths. The depth of water, Franklin told him, was never less than about eight feet. Looking ahead, he could see a gap in the reef a little way to the north, with the usual breakers between it and the shore. But here, opposite the bungalow, the barrier gave complete protection. It would be the perfect place to pick Kastella up, Conway thought—if the opportunity ever came!

They spent a fascinating hour pottering about the reef, observing through the plate glass the lumps of living coral, like enormous delicately tinted brains; and black, foot-long sea cucumbers, and purple sea urchins, and brilliantly hued fish. Then Franklin rowed them back to the beach, and they all went in for a swim. Afterward they lay on rugs in a patch of shade under a palm, and Wendy Franklin began to tell them about an alarming experience one of the "boys" had had with a barracuda the previous year.

Suddenly Franklin pointed along the beach. "There's the emperor," he said, "if you're interested. Taking up his usual pitch."

Leanda turned her head sharply. Conway's gaze swiveled round more slowly. A very large man in a white straw hat and a pair of white shorts was setting up a deck chair about seventy yards away. At that distance they could see nothing of his face. When he had placed the chair to his satisfaction he took some papers from a brief case and sat down with his back to the bathing party.

FOR LEANDA

Leanda said, a little breathlessly, "Doesn't he ever try to talk to *you*?"

"No, he keeps very much to himself."

"What's happened to his bodyguard?"

"Oh, Bates doesn't come down unless he's told to. The master mustn't be disturbed, you know!"

Conway said, "He's a much bigger man than the original emperor."

"Enormous fellow, isn't he. It's odd—I always thought the people of Spyros were an undersized lot."

Leanda was still gazing along the beach. Wendy Franklin said, "Well, I don't know about you people, but I'm thirsty. . . . Shall we go in?"

"Good idea," Franklin said. "It's about time for a snorter."

They picked up their belongings and set off up the path that wound through the trees to the house. Leanda was talking gaily to Wendy. Suddenly, when they'd almost reached the veranda, she stopped short. "Oh, damn, I've left my sunglasses. . . . You go on, I shan't be a moment."

"I'll get them. . . ." Franklin began—but Leanda was already halfway down the path, and running.

"You'd better go, Tom," Wendy said. "She may not be able to find them."

"She'll find them all right," Conway said, putting his hand detainingly on Franklin's arm. "They're by the tree—I saw them. What was that you said about a drink, old boy?"

Franklin hesitated, then gave a little shrug. Leanda was just disappearing down the slope, still running.

Wendy said, "What it is to be only twenty-three! You know,

A HERO

Mr. Cornford, I think your wife's quite charming."

"Hear, hear!" Franklin said enthusiastically. "We're both lucky men!" he added with a grin.

"A shade late, darling," Wendy said. "Is she English, Mr. Cornford?—she's so very dark."

"Welsh," Conway said. "She's a Welsh witch, actually!"

"Only in the nicest sense, I'm quite sure," Wendy said. She looked anxiously down the path. "You know, Tom, she *can't* find them—you really should have gone."

Suddenly Leanda reappeared. She waved to them, holding up the glasses, and slowed to a walk.

"Sorry about that," she said, as she joined them. She avoided Conway's eye, but he could sense her excitement. "Now I could do with a shower."

In their room, Leanda closed the door and turned jubilantly on Conway. "I *did* it, Mike! I'll never forget his face as long as I live. He looked absolutely staggered."

"I should think so." Conway was almost as excited as she was. "What happened?"

"I ran straight up to him and said we'd come to rescue him and could he be down on the beach at midnight? I talked to him in our own language—otherwise I honestly don't think he'd have believed me. But he was very quick—he cottoned on at once, and nodded, and I ran straight back. That's all. Oh, Mike, you can't *imagine* how I feel."

"Better have your shower," Conway said, "and cool off!"

Leanda wanted to go with Conway to keep the appointment when the time came, but he argued against it. The hot night and

92

the need for a breath of air could easily explain the sudden desire of one person to go down to the beach after the household
had retired, he said, but if they both went, and anyone happened to see or hear them, it might seem a little strange. In any
case, he could make the necessary arrangements with Kastella
more quickly on his own. In the end Leanda agreed, reluctantly.

At twelve, Conway put on his dressing gown and slippers and
moved soundlessly to the veranda door. Leanda called a whispered "Good luck!" and he raised his hand in acknowledgment.
Outside on the veranda he stood listening for a moment. Everything seemed quiet. There was a subdued glow of light coming
round the end of the building—the Franklins evidently still had
their room light on. But that shouldn't matter. Conway turned
to the left, away from the light, past the unoccupied bedrooms.
The wooden floor of the veranda creaked slightly under his
tread. After a moment he reached the outer door, turned the key
softly, and let himself out, closing the door behind him.

There was no moon, but the stars were bright enough to light
the way. The noise of cicadas and frogs and the distant roar of
the surf covered the sound of his movements. He glanced across
at Kastella's bungalow. There was a light in one of the front
rooms, but the rest of the house was in darkness. He turned down
the path to the beach, moving at a saunter, as though he were
genuinely taking the air. He reached the beach and turned to the
right along the sand, keeping close to the edge of the trees. He
had covered a little over fifty yards when, from a patch of darkness, a man spoke. The voice was soft, the language strange.

Conway stopped. "Kastella! Where are you?" He groped his
way forward, and touched a foot, and dropped down on the sand

beside it. "Well, thank God you made it . . . ! My name's Conway."

"You're English!" It sounded like an accusation.

"I am not. I'm Irish."

"Ah! Who is the girl? We had no time to talk."

"An ardent supporter of yours," Conway said. "A fellow countryman."

"I know that. Her name!"

"Her name's Leanda Sophoulis."

"She spoke of rescue. How?"

"We have a yacht," Conway said. "We sailed here from Kenya —just the two of us. We're taking you back there. Everything's laid on."

"What is your interest in the matter?"

"I'm being well paid."

"By whom?"

"By Victor Metaxas."

"Metaxas!" For a moment, Kastella was silent. Then he said, "How do I know you are speaking the truth?"

"About what?" Conway asked, with a touch of impatience.

"I have enemies, who would pay a great deal to have me abducted and killed."

"Well, I'm afraid you'll have to take a chance on our genuineness. We've no credentials."

"Is your ship safe? Are you a good seaman?"

"We got here," Conway said. "I guess we can get back."

"My life is valuable. My countrymen depend on me."

"Look," Conway said, "you don't *have* to come. If you'd sooner stay here, just say the word."

94

"Of course I don't want to stay here. For months I have thought of nothing but when I would get away. . . . All right, I must trust your good faith and skill. What do you propose?"

"Can you come here tomorrow night—but a little later, say at one o'clock?"

"If everything is quiet and normal I can do that, yes."

"Good. Then that's all you have to do. There's no need to bring anything with you—we've got all you'll need on board. Is your room at the front of the bungalow?"

"Yes."

"Then leave your light on. See that it's on all the evening—it'll guide us in. If anything goes wrong, if either we or you can't make the rendezvous tomorrow, the same arrangement will hold for the next night, and the next, and so on until we meet. . . . All right?"

"Yes."

"That's all, then. One o'clock tomorrow night, at this spot. I'll be seeing you." Conway got to his feet and walked slowly off along the beach. In a few moments he was back in the house.

As he entered the bedroom, Leanda called out in an eager whisper, "Did you find him?"

"Yes."

"Everything all right?"

"Well," Conway said slowly, "he's a bit long on suspicion and short on gratitude. But I think it's in the bag."

They said good-by to Wendy Franklin in the morning, uncomfortably aware that they too would seem short on gratitude very soon but unable to do anything about it. Tom Franklin drove them back to Port Edward and dropped them at the quay. Conway paid off the boatwatcher and quietly prepared *Thalia* for sea, while Leanda went off to buy fresh food. By midday they were ready to leave—ostensibly for a short fishing trip. They might not be back till the morning, Conway told the harbor master. He started the engine and they motored slowly out along the harbor channel. No one had taken the slightest interest in their departure. At sea, Conway turned the ship away from La Pleasaunce, waiting until they were well away from the land before making a wide sweep to the south. Then he gave the tiller to Leanda while he compared the chart with a map of Heureuse they'd bought. The Franklins' estate was marked on the map, and it was a simple matter to fix its position on the chart. It was just over twelve sea miles away. They had all the time in the world.

There were some high-piled clouds which emptied during the afternoon in a torrent of rain, but afterward the sky cleared again. The faint breeze that had sprung up dropped completely, and the sea became as calm as a lake. Conway put out some lines, in case anyone was watching them from the shore, and they cruised slowly along the coast. By dusk, they were two miles off La Pleasaunce. As the sun went down, Conway turned in toward the reef. Presently lights came on ashore, the lights of the three dwellings. Conway throttled down the engine and edged slowly along the seaward side of the reef till he found the pass through the coral that he'd seen the day before. As soon as *Thalia* was safely inside the lagoon he switched off the engine. With Leanda's help he unshipped and launched the dinghy and made its painter fast to the darkened yacht's bows. Then, rowing with

short strokes and taking his time, he towed the yacht noiselessly
to within a hundred yards of the shore. When she was in position
he made the dinghy fast so that it wouldn't bump against the
hull, and anchored *Thalia* lightly with a warp and kedge. . . .
After that, there was nothing to do but wait.

It was a long wait. Leanda was on edge, now that they were
so near the end. They couldn't show a light or speak above a
whisper or move about except with the greatest caution. Conway dozed a little in his bunk and Leanda rested, though she
couldn't sleep. Slowly, the hours passed. Then, at a quarter to
one, Conway lowered himself into the dinghy and sculled it,
silently and expertly, to the shore.

He paused just outside the breaking wavelet, his ears straining
for any unfamiliar sound. The lights in the Franklin bungalow
were out now. So were all the lights in Kastella's place, except
his own. The signs looked good. Conway paddled the dinghy in
with his hands, and waited tensely.

Suddenly a twig cracked among the trees. A figure approached
across the sand, moving with a heavy, stealthy tread. Kastella
in a dressing gown! "Nice work!" Conway whispered, stepping
out and holding the dinghy for him. "Easy, now!" Kastella got
in, and Conway shoved off. They had only an inch or two of
freeboard and he had to scull with care. The shore receded into
the darkness. Very soon Conway caught the loom of *Thalia*
against the stars, and a few strokes took him alongside. He held
the rail while Kastella climbed into the cockpit. Then he made
the dinghy's painter fast to the bows, and passed the kedge to
Leanda, and towed the ship out to the gap in the reef. As soon

97

as he felt the swell he got Leanda to help him haul the dinghy in again, and started the engine. In a few moments they were through the gap, and heading westward at a steady eight knots.

It had been, after all, a piece of cake!

3

They continued to motor at full speed, without lights, putting the greatest possible distance between themselves and Heureuse. Conway stayed at the tiller, concentrating on the tricky passage through the islands. For a while, Leanda and Kastella sat with him in the cockpit, talking of the escape. Kastella was anxious to hear the whole story, and Leanda told him everything, starting with Conway's loss of *Tara* and finishing with their rewarding social activities on Heureuse. She had suddenly become much more voluble—whether from release of tension, or nervousness in the presence of the great man, Conway didn't know. Kastella listened intently, putting a question from time to time in his soft, quick-speaking, authoritative voice. He was particularly interested in the arrangements for getting him into and out of Africa, and Leanda told him about Malindi, and the lagoon, and Ionides' shack, and the agent's certainty that he could smuggle him aboard a ship. The careful plan seemed to satisfy him.

"Well, this has been quite an achievement, Conway," he said at last. "I congratulate you."

"It's not me you should congratulate," Conway said. "If Leanda hadn't taken a chance and rushed back to speak to you on the beach, you'd still be on Heureuse."

"I appreciate that. A big risk for a big result . . . Thank you, Leanda." He paused. "Thank you for myself *and* Spyros. Who knows?—you may have changed history tonight."

"I still can't quite believe it's happened," Leanda said. "We were terribly lucky to . . ."

She broke off as Conway suddenly throttled the engine back and said, in a tense voice, "*Listen!*" They all listened. But everything seemed normal, and after a moment or two he relaxed. "I thought I heard surf," he said. "Sorry—false alarm."

"Perhaps we'd better go below," Leanda said. "I think our talk's worrying you."

"It might be as well," Conway agreed.

Kastella got up, a dark bulk against the sky. As he steadied himself against the rail, *Thalia* rocked. "You'd better lead the way, Leanda," he said. Leanda guided him into the unlit saloon. Conway could hear them talking and laughing as she fixed up a bunk for him. They were using their own language now. After they'd settled down in the bunks they started some new discussion. Kastella's voice was scarcely audible above the beat of the engine but Leanda's carried clearly. There was only one word that Conway understood, a word that constantly recurred—"Spyros." Around three in the morning, as the talk still flowed, he called out, "You should get some sleep, Leanda—there's work ahead." After that there was silence, except for the engine. Alone at the tiller, Conway continued to watch and listen.

Kastella was the first to emerge in the morning. He came up around seven, still wearing his dressing gown, and at last Conway was able to see what he looked like in daylight. His appearance was striking. He was a very tall man, well over six feet, with a powerful frame. He had a massive head, with a wide forehead running back on either side of a widow's peak of thinning dark hair. His nose was large, his mouth tight and finely chiseled, his eyes commanding. He was no Adonis, Conway decided, but he was most distinguished-looking, with the bearing of a leader. His age, Conway thought, was probably about forty-five.

Kastella returned Conway's gaze for a moment or two, making his own calm inspection. Then he said, "Good morning, Conway," in a friendly tone, and sat down in the cockpit.

Conway said, "Did you manage to get some sleep?"

"As much as I needed, thank you." Kastella looked carefully around the horizon. There were low islands lying on both quarters, with coconut palms rising from them. "What sort of progress are we making?"

Conway glanced at the patent log. "We've done forty-eight miles. Another hour or so, and we'll be out of sight of land."

Kastella nodded. "I wonder if they'll try to follow us."

"Nobody saw us leave," Conway said. "Nobody can be sure where we're making for."

"No, but Africa's the nearest place. They'll probably guess we came out this way."

"Nearness isn't everything," Conway said. "I doubt if they'll expect us to go back where we came from."

"We could have been seen at daybreak from one of the outlying copra stations. Most of them are in contact with Heureuse by radio."

"Well, I'd be surprised if there was anything in the island fast enough to catch us now—we've had too long a start. I think we're safe enough."

"Let's hope you're right," Kastella said. "But don't underestimate the English, Conway. They've lost a very important prize in me. They've also been made to look foolish. They're quite capable of sending an aircraft carrier to search for us."

"I don't know where they'd send it from," Conway said. "The nearest must be at least a thousand miles away—and anyhow, the ocean's a hell of a big place to search, even with aircraft."

"All the same, wouldn't it be a sensible precaution to turn off the direct track for a while—just in case?"

"Don't worry," Conway said. "That's what I intend to do."

Presently Leanda stuck her head out of the saloon. "Morning, Mike!" she called cheerfully. "Morning, Mr. Kastella!"

" 'Alex,' to you," Kastella said. "We really can't have formalities in a small boat."

She smiled. "Very well . . . Sorry I've been so lazy, Mike."

"You'll be making up for it later," Conway said.

"I won't be long. . . ." She went below to dress. Above the noise of the engine, Conway could hear her singing. Kastella was listening, too.

"One of our folk songs . . ." he said. He moved nearer the door.

"What a delightful voice she has!"

"I never heard it before," Conway said. "I guess she's got more to sing about now."

In a few moments she was back on deck. "Alex, you'd better come and collect the things we brought for you from Mombasa —I'm sure you'd like to get out of that dressing gown. You can use the forecabin while I get breakfast. . . ."

"What have we got for breakfast?" Conway asked.

"Orange juice. Tinned bacon, tinned sausages, fresh eggs. Coffee. All right?"

"Sounds wonderful," Conway said.

They were clearing the land, now, and a faint breeze was stirring the smooth surface of the sea. Presently Conway turned off the engine and hoisted the sails. The wind was heading them a little, but *Thalia* still had a good slant. He stayed at the tiller while Leanda cooked breakfast, enjoying the quiet chuckle of the water under the bows and the engineless peace. He could even hear the bacon sizzling in the pan. At his suggestion, Leanda ate first, with Kastella; then he gave her the tiller and went below, while Kastella sat beside her in the cockpit, still talking. They were continuing to use the liquid, flowing language of their country. Once or twice, as Leanda caught Conway's eye through the open saloon door, she switched to English, trying to bring him into the conversation, but Kastella always switched back.

After breakfast Conway and Leanda started the old routine of the ship's chores while Kastella shaved in the saloon. His presence had the effect of slowing everything down a great deal.

103

He was too bulky a man to make a comfortable third in so small a yacht, and whatever part of the ship he was in seemed crowded. Also, by constantly talking to Leanda, he distracted her, so that Conway had to remind her once or twice of things not done. But by noon the decks had been washed down, a supply of water filtered and made drinkable, the log written up, and the first sights taken. Kastella was interested in all that went on, and asked a good many questions. It was clear that he knew next to nothing about sailing or boats, but he seemed willing to learn.

At two, they picked up their first news bulletin, from the small radio station on Heureuse. The story was out, but the information was thin. All the announcer said was that Kastella had disappeared overnight from the bungalow where he had been living, and that a search was being made throughout the island. No mention was made of *Thalia*.

"Official discretion!" Kastella said, as Leanda switched off and they rejoined Conway in the cockpit. "Would I have run off into the bush in pajamas and a dressing gown? We must listen again."

"I suppose they're trying to make up their minds what to say," Leanda said. "Can you imagine what a state they must be in!"

Kastella chuckled. "They used to call me 'the emperor,' you know—a silly title, but it amused them. I doubt if it occurred to anyone that their little island might become an Elba! It's a pleasing thought."

Conway said, "I suppose Sergeant Bates is a constable again by now!"

FOR LEANDA

They sailed on all day in a quiet sea. It was much hotter than it had been on the outward journey, and the saloon was stifling. Leanda was wearing the minimum of clothes, and Kastella had stripped down to cotton swimming trunks, revealing a magnificent, bronzed body that made Conway's muscular torso look almost puny. Conway had promised to give him some sailing lessons when they'd got a little further from Heureuse, but at the moment there was nothing for him to do and he spent a good deal of time in Leanda's old place, up on the foredeck, where he was out of the way and could catch all the breeze there was. Leanda and Conway were again standing regular watches. Leanda was having a bit more difficulty with the yacht now, for the breeze was fickle, changing both its direction and its strength without warning. But mainly it was light, and Conway was able to leave her for a while in the afternoon, and get some sleep. When he checked the log at six, he found they had covered thirty-seven miles in their twelve hours of daylight sailing. Star sights put them some miles short of that—the east-going current that had helped them so much on the way out was now against them. But he felt reasonably satisfied. A northwesterly course had taken them well away from the direct approaches to Heureuse, and the sea around them was empty.

Kastella helped Leanda prepare the supper, and they had the usual two-service meal. Afterward, as the three of them sat in the cockpit, Kastella raised the subject of the night's arrangements. "Where would you like me to go?" he asked.

"You'd better take the forecabin for the time being," Conway said.

"Really?" Kastella looked a little surprised. "I'd have thought Leanda should have the forecabin. It is, after all, the only place with any privacy."

"I'll be wanting her help," Conway said shortly. "I'd sooner have her handy."

"But she can easily reach you from the forecabin whenever you want her. It seems to me by far the most sensible arrangement. . . . You'd prefer the forecabin, Leanda, wouldn't you?"

Leanda glanced at Conway. "Mike's the boss," she said. "Anyway we're both used to the saloon."

Kastella shrugged. "Very well—though it does seem to me an inconvenient arrangement." After a moment he got up and went below to stow his things.

Conway said, "What's his idea?" in a fierce tone.

"He was only trying to be considerate, Mike."

"Well, he'd better mind his own business—I'm not going to have him interfering in the running of the ship."

"Of course not—but I'm sure he meant well. There's nothing to be cross about. . . . Oh, Mike, isn't it wonderful that we've got away!"

The wind continued light throughout the night, and the alternating watches went smoothly. Conway had quite recovered his equanimity, now that Kastella was safely out of the way, and he spent the greater part of one of his two-hour off-duty spells sitting contentedly beside Leanda under the stars. By morning they had clocked another twenty-six miles. Conway decided that they were simply wasting time by continuing on a northwesterly course any longer, and turned *Thalia's* head due west again. Even Kastella, when he appeared on deck at seven, agreed that the emptiness of the ocean was reassuring. He seemed to be in a very amiable mood. After breakfast he asked to be given a job, and Conway gave him the mop and bucket and let him swab the decks down while Leanda cleared up below. Then, since the breeze was steady, Conway called him to the tiller and for an hour instructed him patiently in the theory and practice of sailing. Kastella absorbed the theory quickly, and showed quite a bit of practical skill. His main trouble was over-confidence—a tendency to go his own way and respond too slowly to Conway's instructions. Several times the big mainsail swung over in a light jibe as Kastella's erratic steering put the wind behind the boom. But on the whole Conway found him promising, and said so. "We'll all be sharing watches before the end of this trip," he prophesied. "You must keep at it."

For a while, after lunch, Kastella retired to his cabin to do some writing. Then, at two o'clock, they tuned in again to Radio Heureuse. This time, Kastella's disappearance took up almost the whole of the bulletin. There was no more talk of an island search. The marks of a rowing boat had been found in the sand below the bungalow, the announcer said, and it was now believed that Kastella had been taken off in a yacht named *Thalia*, owned by a Mr. and Mrs. Michael Cornford, which had arrived a few days earlier from Mombasa and had left without proper clearance shortly before the disappearance was reported. Inquiries in Mombasa, the bulletin said, had revealed that the yacht had been purchased only a week or two before. The former owner, a well-known Mombasa businessman named Paul Ionides, had told a news agency that he had bought it as a speculation and had sold it in good faith to a couple who had answered an advertisement he had inserted in an English yachting journal. They had said they were going for a holiday cruise, and he'd had no idea at all that they intended to use it for any nefarious purpose.

Kastella frowned a little over the last item. "*Did* he put an advertisement in an English yachting paper?" he asked.

"You bet he did," Conway said. "He and Metaxas between them thought of just about everything."

"His Spyros-sounding name is bound to make people wonder. The Kenya police may well think he was involved."

"If they do, they can't prove anything. Ionides has got documents to back up his story all the way through. Anyhow, the more they suspect him, the less likely they'll be to think we'll go back there. I'm sure you've nothing to worry about."

Kastella grunted. After a moment he turned the radio dial to the short-wave band and found other stations where the escape was being discussed. It had obviously caused a tremendous sensation, and was top news everywhere. Most of the interest seemed to be in where *Thalia* was making for. A French station thought it probable that the yacht was heading for India, where Kastella could be pretty sure of political asylum. A Dutch station suggested Ceylon. No one mentioned Kenya as a possible refuge. An American commentator reported that London was "stunned" by the news, and very concerned about the effect the escape had already had in Spyros. It seemed that a new wave of terrorism had swept over the colony, resulting in the deaths of three policemen and five terrorists.

Kastella switched off the radio in sudden anger. "Idiots!" he exclaimed. "Worse than idiots! *They're* not winning freedom, they're sabotaging it."

"They don't realize that," Leanda said. She looked a bit shaken, too.

"Some of them do. I could name a few, and so could you. So could our friend Metaxas. Men who look on violence as a short cut to power."

Conway said, "It often has been."

"This time it won't be—not if I can help it."

"What do you plan to do," Conway asked, "supposing you get the chance?"

"I plan to form an orderly and democratic government in a free and independent Spyros, Conway. . . . *If* I can ever get the English to realize where their true interests lie."

Conway said, "Well, it sounds all right!"

The afternoon passed quietly. There was a little excitement about three o'clock, when Conway suddenly spotted a sail on the starboard beam, but it was only a small fishing ketch from one of the islands and it soon faded into the blue of the horizon. Otherwise they saw nothing. Kastella had another spell at the tiller and then returned to his perch in the bows. Leanda, between watches, was absorbed in some document that Kastella had given her to read.

In the late afternoon the wind backed to the southeast, and strengthened, and the idling yacht suddenly came to life. For the first time in all the hundreds of miles since Mombasa she was sailing free in a fresh breeze and she fairly raced through the water. The calm sea quickly became choppy. Leanda abandoned her reading and restowed some things that were banging about in one of the lockers. Conway, thinking they might be in for a real blow, called to her to have a look at the barometer, but she reported that it was steady. For a while he watched the waves surging against the hull and wondered if he would have to take in a reef. Spray was beginning to shoot up over the bows as the yacht dipped in the shallow troughs. Kastella looked back, grinning, and waved. Suddenly the boat dipped into a steeper trough than usual, and Kastella grabbed hold of the pulpit as a considerable weight of water swept over the foredeck.

Conway called, "Better come down, Kastella!"

Kastella waved again, but didn't move.

Conway shouted, "Kastella!—come down!" A gust caught the sail, and *Thalia* heeled sharply. A fresh torrent of water shot over the bows. After a moment, Kastella got up and slowly made his way to the cockpit.

"You take your time, don't you?" Conway said.

Kastella looked at him in surprise. "I was perfectly all right. There was no need to panic."

"Panic, my foot! Some seas are bigger than others, that's all— and they don't ring a bell when they're coming. You're perishable cargo, and it's my job to look after you."

"I appreciate your concern," Kastella said, "but it really isn't necessary. I'm not a child, you know." He glanced at Leanda, and smiled, and went below.

Leanda looked unhappily at Conway. "Mike, you don't have to be so short-tempered. I'm sure he *was* all right."

"Maybe he was, maybe he wasn't," Conway said. "Anyway, that's not the point."

They had a fine sail through the night and by dawn next morning they were nearly two hundred miles from Port Edward —but now the fickle weather changed once more. The wind died completely, and the sea quickly subsided. By noon it was as smooth as oiled silk. *Thalia's* log line hung straight down in the translucent water. Sea and sky merged in a haze of heat. The deck became uncomfortable for bare feet. Conway tapped the glass again—and made a face. Presently he furled the sails, and rigged an awning over the cockpit.

Kastella said, "Why don't we use the engine?"

"I want to save our fuel," Conway told him.

"But surely this is just the time to use it. Every day is important to me, Conway—and not only to me. We must get on."

"Look," Conway said, "we've eight hundred miles to go and we've fuel for about four hundred miles, so we can't motor all the way. If we use it up now, we won't have it later when we may need it more. At the moment, I prefer to wait for wind."

"It may be a long wait," Kastella said.

"It won't be. The glass has fallen a tenth, and that's a lot for these parts. By tonight there'll be more wind than we want."

"Then isn't that another reason for making steady progress while we can?"

"Oh, for Christ's sake, stop arguing!" Conway burst out. "I'm going to get some sleep."

111

The afternoon was grilling. The sun beat down from a cloudless sky, turning the motionless ship into an oven. Sleep, Conway discovered, was impossible. The moment he lay down in the stifling cabin he was in a bath of sweat. The drinking water, which Leanda was making in far greater quantities than ever before, was too warm to quench thirst properly. The air was leaden. Even Leanda, who usually contrived to look cool, was wilting visibly.

Around three, she suddenly said, "Mike, will you come and swim with me?"

Conway grinned. "With you and the sharks?"

"It'll be safe enough if we splash. Just round the ship."

He hesitated. "It's certainly an attractive idea. . . ."

Kastella said, "I think it's a splendid idea. . . . Come on, Leanda, get your things off." He added something in their own language, which made her flush and smile a little.

Conway said curtly, "You two go. I'll keep watch."

"Oh, come on, Mike," Leanda coaxed him. She had already slipped off her light clothes and substituted an exiguous swim suit. "Just for a few minutes."

"I'd sooner stay and watch," he said. "You carry on—but keep close in. And when you're ready to come back, use the rudder. It's the only way to climb up."

She still looked disappointed, but she didn't say anything more. Conway watched them dive in. Then he fetched the shotgun from the forecabin and mounted guard on the coach roof, his eyes alert for the first sign of a black fin. But nothing appeared. For ten minutes the swimmers circled the ship, laughing and splashing and calling to Conway that he was missing the swim of his life. Then he helped to haul them aboard and they went below to change. Conway sat down under the awning. He could still hear them talking and laughing. Suddenly, music filled the ship, as someone switched on the radio. Conway stirred restlessly. The music continued. After it had been going for some time, he called out, "Leanda!"

She came to the cabin door.

"Better switch that thing off," he said.

She nodded, and went back into the saloon. In a moment, Kastella's head appeared. "Surely we can have a little music?" he said.

"I'm afraid not. I don't want to run the battery down."

"It seems well charged," Kastella said.

"It needs to be. If that battery goes flat I shan't be able to check the chronometer. If I can't check the chronometer I shan't be able to fix our position."

"All right—I'll turn it off when the program stops."

Conway scrambled to his feet. "You'll turn it off now!" he said. For a moment, the two men faced each other. Kastella, three stone heavier and two inches taller, was arrogantly calm. Conway's fists were clenched in the recklessness of pent-up anger. Then the music stopped, as Leanda turned the switch.

Kastella said, "Aren't you rather forgetting yourself, Conway?"

"What the hell do you mean by that?"

"May I remind you that you're a hired man—and that you're being paid to take me to Africa, not to give me orders. I don't take orders from anyone—least of all from you."

Leanda, pale and distressed, said, "Alex—*please!*"

113

Conway took a deep breath. "Well," he said, "I guess this is the showdown. Now let me tell *you* something, Kastella. You may be an emperor in your own estimation, but you're not in mine. To me, you're just a fugitive, and a pretty useless one. I'm the master of this ship, and in everything that concerns the ship you *will* take my orders. What's more, you'll jump to it. Otherwise . . ."

Kastella said softly, "Otherwise *what*, Mr. Conway?"

"Otherwise you can bloody well sail yourself to Africa," Conway said. "And that I mean."

It was Leanda who acted as peacemaker. For an hour she was with Kastella in the forecabin. Then, just before dusk, she came out to Conway in the cockpit and sat down beside him.

"Mike, I want to talk to you."

"That's a nice change," he said.

"Mike, please don't be silly. Kastella's sorry about—all that."

"So he damn well should be."

"I dare say, but you must try to understand him. He *isn't* used to taking orders, he's used to giving them. I know he seems interfering and overbearing, but you've got to make some allowances. He's not an ordinary man—he's really a very great man."

"You don't have to interpret him to me," Conway said. "I can see very well what he is—and he doesn't seem great to me. . . . Damn it, Leanda, any fool should know that you can't have divided command in a ship."

"Of course you can't, and he admits it."

"Naturally he admits it now—because he knows he can't get to Africa without me."

114

"It's not only that—he really does admit it. But you made him angry, because of the way you spoke to him. You *have* been short-tempered, you know, ever since we started this trip back. You must agree that most of the disputes have been over very trifling things."

"Okay," Conway said, "I'm bad-tempered."

"You're not, really, but it's hot, and Kastella's difficult, and you don't like three in a ship."

"I don't when you concentrate on one to the exclusion of the other."

"Oh, Mike, I try not to—honestly, I do. But Kastella and I have so much in common—so many things to talk about. He's been telling me all about his plans for Spyros—he talks wonderfully—it's tremendously exciting for me. It's just as though everything I've worked for was going to come true. You can't imagine what it's like. . . ."

"If you talked in English," Conway said, "I might get some inkling."

"I'd sooner talk in English, but I can't if he starts the other way, and he hates using it when he doesn't have to. . . . Anyway, that isn't really very important, is it? Mike, we've got to make a fresh start, all of us. This trip is going to be absolute hell if you two are at loggerheads—you've *got* to make it up."

"Then he'd better apologize!"

"Mike, you know he won't do that—any more than you will. You're both proud and pigheaded. He's—well, an emperor, if you like—and you're an Irishman! Now do be sensible, *please!*" She put her hand on his. "Meet him halfway."

"What do you call halfway?"

"He'll take your orders. You'll give them nicely."

Conway looked down at her pleading face—and slowly he smiled. "Well, that sounds fair enough, I must say. . . . You're quite a diplomat, aren't you?"

She sighed. "I need to be!" she said.

By evening, it was clear to all of them that a violent change in the weather was imminent. The sun went down in a sickly, yellowish-green sky. The sea looked oily and sinister. To the south, great black and purple clouds were piling up like an atomic mushroom. Conway took three careful star sights before darkness finally closed in, and got a good fix. Then he made a round of the ship, seeing that the forehatch was tightly closed, the ports screwed up, and the contents of the lockers well chocked. Kastella, amiable again after their reconciliation and anxious to lend a hand, helped him put an extra lashing on the dinghy. Afterward, Conway went forward to the forepeak and brought up two long warps, and the sea anchor.

Kastella looked curiously at the conical canvas bag, with its iron ring sewn at the mouth. "What's it for, Conway?"

"To ride to if the wind gets too strong," Conway told him. "Or to slow the ship down if we have to run before the wind."

"Why does she have to be slowed down?"

"If the ship goes faster than the following seas, the waves break over her stern. If she goes slower, they pass harmlessly underneath. We hope!"

"And will this thing really hold her back?"

"It will indeed. It's got a terrific drag in the water." Conway put it on one of the bunks, just inside the saloon door. "Leanda, what about making a flask of coffee while we're still on an even keel. . . . I advise Dramamine for all hands, too!"

He went out into the cockpit and inspected the menacing cloud mass that was steadily rolling up from the south. It looked horrible. The glass was still falling. The air was like a clammy hand. He had already close-reefed the mainsail and bent on the small jib, but now he decided it would be wiser not to risk light canvas at all. He climbed to the coach roof and lashed the sail to the boom and the boom securely down. Then he fetched the heavy trysail and storm jib, with their strong bolt ropes and fittings, and bent those on instead.

The storm broke with staggering suddenness. At one moment, all was calm and quiet; the next, a vivid fork of lightning split the sky, and the heavens opened. In the cockpit, it was like sitting under a warm waterfall. Leanda and Kastella dived for the cabin; Conway, still wearing nothing but shorts, let the water pour off him, and watched the storm. The downpour continued for half an hour, with incessant lightning and crashing thunder. Then, as the rain stopped, a wind came howling out of the south. Conway grabbed the trysail's double sheet, the sail filled, and in a moment *Thalia* was racing away at top speed. Conway braced himself against the gunwale, shaking the water out of his eyes. It was good to be sailing again, whatever was in store. This was going to be *Thalia's* real test, and he hadn't a doubt she would come through it well. Already he had an owner's pride in her.

The wind increased steadily, backing to the east, and whipping up a big sea. *Thalia's* motion became lively, and dollops of spray started coming over into the cockpit. Nasty-looking seas

117

began rolling up astern. Conway steered carefully, meeting them exactly stern on, watching for any sign of a jibe. Still the wind strengthened. Soon it was blowing at force seven, and they were beginning to make too much speed for safety. Conway pulled the jib to windward, hauled in the mainsheet, and lashed the helm halfway. He wanted to see how *Thalia* would lie hove to to, though he hadn't any great expectations. In fact she heeled alarmingly, and much more water came aboard. He climbed to the coach roof and got the sails off her, fighting the wind. *Thalia* turned broadside on, bobbing about like a cork. Water was breaking over the deck. Conway fetched the sea anchor and streamed it over the weather bow. *Thalia* still refused to ride comfortably. Waves were pounding against her side with shattering violence. He tripped the anchor and hauled it in. He'd expected to have to run before it, anyway. He clambered back to the cockpit, with the wind shrieking round his ears, and streamed his two heavy warps from the stern, with cushions and fenders and bundles of old rope tied to the ends. Then he streamed the sea anchor, too.

By now it was blowing a fresh gale, and more in the gusts. The sea was a wild, tossing waste. The air was thick with flying spray. But *Thalia* was lying comfortably at last, stern on to the wind and seas. With the long warps helping to check her progress, the strain on the sea anchor was well short of breaking point. If the storm grew no worse, the ship would drive safely before the wind all night. She had nearly seven hundred miles of sea room to leeward, and not a shoal anywhere.

There was nothing more that Conway could do, and presently he went below to see how his crew and passenger were faring.

The noise in the saloon was infinitely worse than on deck. Every few seconds there was a frightful, shuddering jar as the bows fell from the top of a sea into a trough. The incessant shocks were felt almost like physical blows on the body. The clamor of the water against the thin planking was indescribable. Kastella, in the forecabin, was in a pretty bad way, judging by the sounds. Conway hoped he had taken a bucket in with him. Lear 'a was lying face down on one of the saloon bunks, her head cushioned in her arms. She looked up as Conway entered, and gave him a wan smile. "Are we all right?" she asked.

"Sure we're all right! Why?—feeling scared?"

"A little . . . I never imagined anything like this."

"There's nothing whatever to worry about."

"I wanted to come out and help, but I couldn't. . . ." It suddenly dawned on her that there was no one at the tiller. "What's happening?"

"She's running under bare poles, with the sea anchor out. She'll be all right. . . ." For a moment his hand rested reassuringly on Leanda's hair. "You don't look too bad."

"My head feels pretty awful—but I could be worse."

"Is there anything you want?"

"I'd love some water. I don't think I could get up."

Conway drew a mugful, and gave it to her. Then he stretched out on the other bunk. There was no question of sleep, or even rest. The roar of the wind was deafening. In the gusts it rose to an insane shriek in the rigging. The little ship kept going up like a lift, and then falling with a crunch into the hollows. The battering ram of the water never ceased. Conway lay listening, noting every change of sound or movement, ready to rush into

119

the cockpit on the instant if necessary. There was a second sea anchor in the forepeak if the first one split or carried away; there were more spare warps. But nothing happened. With luck, nothing would happen. The long night had to be endured, sweated out, and that was all. He had known far worse conditions. It was better down here, running with the gale, than up at the tiller trying desperately to claw off a lee shore, as he'd once had to do in *Tara*.

Around three in the morning the wind veered to the south-east again, making the sea even more confused and *Thalia's* motion harder to bear. Conway forced his way out on deck and had a look round. The sea anchor was doing its work well—very little water was being shipped, and the self-draining cockpit was dealing with all there was. The gale was still blowing with great fury, but it was no worse. He stood there for a while with his back pressed against the cabin bulkhead, watching the green phosphorescent fire that poured down the slopes of the huge waves. Then he staggered back into the saloon, and drank some coffee from the flask, and stretched out on his bunk again.

It blew all night without a moment's respite, and far into the day. Apart from Conway's occasional sorties, no one made any move. There was nothing to be done, nothing to be gained by trying to walk about. An occasional groan was the only sound from the forecabin. Conway offered Leanda the rest of the coffee, but she shook her head in silent misery. It wasn't until well after midday that the wind began to take off a little and the sea to moderate. Then everyone fell into an exhausted sleep. When Conway woke, it was nearly four o'clock. Stiff and bruised, he went outside to look at the weather. The wind had fallen to a gentle breeze, and the sun was shining. The sea was still heaving after the storm, but all the viciousness had gone out of it. *Thalia*, without any canvas to steady her, was rolling uneasily in the swell.

Leanda was awake when he returned to the saloon. A little color had crept back into her cheeks, and she smiled at him.

"Better?" he asked.

"Much better . . . Mike, I thought I should die! Is that what you call the doldrums?"

Conway chuckled. He was feeling on pretty good terms with himself. "I'd say that gale was a bit of a freak. All those atom bombs, you know!"

They began to straighten up the disorder in the saloon. Presently Kastella appeared. His face looked gray, but he managed a feeble grin. "Well, are we still afloat?" he said.

"Yes, and the right way up!"

"It's hard to believe. . . . What an absolutely dreadful night!"

"We did get quite a pasting," Conway said.

Kastella ran a hand through his disheveled hair. "I'm sorry I couldn't give you any help."

"There was nothing to do," Conway said. "The wind took charge, and we just blew."

"Not back toward Heureuse, I hope?"

"No, away from it."

"Ah!" Kastella looked relieved. "As long as we're still making progress . . . Where do you think we are?"

"I'll be able to tell you at dusk," Conway said. "Now let's have some food—I'm ravenous."

While Leanda prepared the meal, Conway stowed the sea

121

anchor and warps and squared up on deck. By the time they'd eaten, the sun was beginning to go down. As the sky darkened and the first stars came out, Conway took sights from the uneasily rolling cockpit and worked out a rough position. They had been carried just over ninety miles during the twenty-four hours, in a direction slightly north of west.

There was still enough light in the cockpit for the final chores. The ship was out of drinking water, and Leanda brought the filter bags and box of chemical cubes into the cockpit to make a fresh supply, while Kastella did the washing up in the galley and Conway prepared to get under way. The wind was light and very uncertain again, but it seemed to be mainly from the east. Conway freed the sheet and hoisted the sail and the boom swung slowly out to starboard. He returned to the tiller and hauled in the sheet and the sail filled. They were away.

The disaster that followed was totally unexpected. Conway felt the boom lift as the wind shifted behind the sail. He just failed to prevent a jibe, but it wasn't a serious one. The boom swung over quite gently, well clear of Leanda's head. She was standing by the port rail, taking a chemical cube from the box. She ducked to avoid the sheet, but the slack of it tangled with her. A moment later the box of chemicals had been jerked from her hand and carried over the side.

The instant Conway realized what had happened he let go of the sheet and tiller and leaped for the gunwale. But the box had already disappeared, swallowed up in the dark sea. For a second he continued to gaze down in horror. Then he turned to Leanda. "My God," he said softly, "that's done it!"

"Mike, I wasn't expecting it. . . ." She stood biting her lips, trying not to cry. "Oh, Mike, what are we going to do?"

Kastella appeared in the lighted doorway of the saloon. "What's the trouble, Leanda?"

"I've dropped all the cubes into the sea—the things we use to make drinking water."

"Well, we've got some other water, I suppose."

"Five gallons," Conway said, "in the emergency tank."

"*Five gallons!* You mean that's all—in the whole ship?"

"A little less, if anything. I used some during the night."

Kastella's face darkened with anger. "My God, what folly!" He turned venomously on Leanda. "Do you realize what your clumsiness may cost us?"

"Shut up!" Conway said roughly. "It wasn't Leanda's fault. It was mine if it was anybody's—I should have foreseen it. . . . Anyway, it's done. Cursing isn't going to help."

There was a short silence. Then Kastella said in a quieter tone, "How long will five gallons last us?"

"It depends on the weather. . . . Four or five days, perhaps. Maybe six, with a bit of discomfort."

"And we've seven hundred miles to go."

Conway stared at him. "You surely don't imagine we can go on?"

"Of course we must go on."

Conway shook his head. "It's out of the question."

"But we've no alternative, Conway. We'll have to make a dash for it—use the engine to get as far as possible as quickly as possible, and hope for rain to eke out our water at the end of the trip."

"You're crazy," Conway said. "We've fuel for two days' steaming—say four hundred miles. That would still leave us three hundred miles out in the ocean. We'd be at the mercy of the doldrums—which could easily mean no progress and no rain. We certainly couldn't *count* on rain. Remember what it was like before the storm—a blistering flat calm? In these latitudes you can spend days like that. Weeks, if you're unlucky."

"We'll have to risk that. . . . Leanda, you agree, don't you—*you* know how important it is."

"You're wasting your breath," Conway said. "To try and cross this ocean with five gallons of water for three people would be only just short of suicide—and a damned unpleasant death it could be, too! Good God, man, I can drink two gallons a day on my own when it's very hot—and still feel thirsty. You must be off your head."

Leanda said, "I read somewhere about a man who drank ordinary sea water for quite a long time, and survived. . . ."

"He was a superman. *We're* not going to drink sea water. And we're definitely not going on."

"Then what *are* we going to do?" Kastella asked. "You're not suggesting we go back to Heureuse!"

"I shouldn't think that'll be necessary," Conway said. "Just a moment while I get these sails off—then we'll have a look at the chart."

He cleared up on deck and then joined the others in the saloon. Leanda had already found the chart of the islands and spread it out on the table. Conway studied it for a while in silence, watched broodingly by Kastella.

"Well," he said at last, "my suggestion is that we make for

Victoria." He indicated a small island on the northwestern edge of the group. "It's the nearest bit of land to us—I make it about two hundred and thirty miles—and there's a copra trading station there. That means water."

"It also means a radio station," Kastella said, "and an English manager who'll know all about me, and about this ship, and who'll have a staff to do what he tells them. Far from getting any water, we shouldn't be allowed to leave."

"If we timed our arrival properly we wouldn't be seen," Conway said. "I'm not proposing we should sail straight up to the jetty in daylight! We'd have to go in at night, and anchor in some quiet spot off the coast, and do a bit of prospecting. With luck we might easily find a well on the edge of the settlement. Even if we only found a stream or a pond, it would do—we could always boil the stuff."

"What would we carry it in?" Leanda asked. "We haven't got anything on board except buckets, and that would mean a lot of journeys. And we still wouldn't have anywhere to store it."

"I dare say we'd find something ashore," Conway said. "Some of these native huts have old tanks outside to catch rain water. We'd have to help ourselves."

"And probably rouse the whole place," Kastella said.

"We'd have to be careful."

Kastella slowly shook his head. "I don't like it at all."

"I don't *like* it myself," Conway said. "I've an interest in you, too, don't forget—quite a big one. I'm only suggesting this because I think it's the best hope."

"There's a great risk I'd be caught."

"There's a risk we'd all be caught."

Kastella gave a thin smile. "You don't seem to understand, Conway—for me this isn't just a question of a few weeks in jail for a passport offense. My country's future is at stake. If I were recaptured now, everything might be lost. The failure would have a crushing effect on our cause. It would be worse than if I'd never escaped."

Leanda said, "But, Alex, if there's no alternative . . ."

Kastella looked at Conway. "Give me your honest opinion— what do you think our chances really are of getting enough water for our needs and leaving without being discovered?"

Conway shrugged. "It's a tough question. I don't know what the situation will be. But I'd have thought there was a fifty-fifty chance."

Kastella was silent for a long while. Finally he said, "Well, in that case I suppose we'd better make for Victoria."

The wind freshened a little during the night, and by dawn *Thalia* had logged thirty miles on a northeasterly course. Kastella merely grunted when Conway told him. He was in a black, shut-in mood, and at breakfast he barely spoke. Conway tried to take his mind off their misfortune by calling him to the tiller and giving him another sailing lesson. Surprisingly, he did better than before—so much so that Conway left him to it for an hour, with Leanda watching over him, and spent the time with the island chart, working out the best line of approach to Victoria and planning a provisional timetable. Then the wind gradually died away, and he had to start the engine. They motored all morning over a quiet sea.

It was shortly before noon that Leanda, from the coach roof, suddenly called, "Mike, I think I can see another boat!" and pointed over the port bow. Conway looked ahead in surprise. This was about the last place he'd have expected to meet anything. But Leanda was right—there was a tiny black dot on the sea. Presently he gave the helm to Kastella and went below to get his binoculars.

"She looks like a small fishing boat," he said after a moment. "I wonder what she's doing so far from the banks."

"We'd better keep clear of her," Kastella said.

"Why?—she might be able to let us have some water. Then we wouldn't need to go to Victoria."

Kastella stared at him. Slowly, his face brightened. "That's a good idea, Conway. I hadn't thought of it." He altered course to port, and put on speed.

As the gap narrowed and the boat grew larger, Conway examined her again through the glasses. "She's been in trouble," he said. "Lost her foremast, by the look of it . . ." He continued to study her. "Do you know, I believe she's that ketch we saw soon after we left the islands. She must have been blown out here by the gale."

They closed her rapidly. Now they could see two people in the bows, waving—two Negroes, an elderly man and a younger one. As *Thalia* drew nearer, an enormous Negress appeared from below, with two small children—a boy and a girl. They were all waving madly, and it was easy to see why. The ketch had taken a savage beating. The foremast was snapped off short, leaving a jagged stump. A mere shred of tattered sail dropped from the mizzen. The ship was motionless. Conway steered *Thalia* carefully alongside and passed a line to the

127

elderly Negro, who made it fast. His eyes were bloodshot, and his coal-black face looked gray with tiredness, but his mouth gaped in a huge smile. In a moment he was pouring out a flood of information in an incomprehensible French patois. The only word that Conway could get sounded like "tempête"—and that told him nothing he didn't know.

The little boy's head had a dirty bandage round it, smeared with dried blood. There was blood on his blue cotton shirt, too. Conway said, "What happened to him?" pointing. The Negress said, "Tombé—tempête!" The flow of words started again.

Leanda said, "Don't you think I ought to put a proper dressing on, Mike?—we've got lots of stuff." Conway said, "Good idea!" and held out his arms for the boy and lifted him into *Thalia*. Then he climbed aboard the ketch. The boat was no more than forty feet long, and very ancient. From stem to stern, it was in a state of frightful disorder. Lumps of shark meat were drying in the cockpit, giving off a powerful smell of ammonia. The cabin was piled high with tangled ropes and salvaged gear. The mizzenmast, Conway now saw, was badly split. The mainsail was in ribbons. Conway said, "No more sail?" gesturing with his arms. The Negro shook his head. "Fini, massa—fini."

"What about your engine? Moteur!"

"Fini," the Negro said sadly. "Tout fini."

Conway bent to examine it. It was a petrol engine, a very old one. He tried the starting handle, but nothing moved. He took the dip stick from the sump, and found it dry. The engine was seized up solid.

He got to his feet, frowning, and looked around. "How much water have you got? Water. L'eau." He pretended to drink.

The Negro smiled. "Di leau, oui." He took Conway's arm and led him to the stern. There was a largish tank under the transom, once galvanized but now very rusty. Conway unscrewed the cap and looked in. It was about three-quarters full.

"Good," he said, and replaced the cap. "Wait, now—two minutes." He climbed back aboard *Thalia*. Kastella, who had been watching and listening from *Thalia's* cockpit, said, "Well?" Leanda was just finishing bandaging the little boy's head. Conway held the end while she fixed it with a safety pin. "Is it a bad cut?" he asked.

"It's quite nasty, poor little kid, but it should be all right if they look after him. . . . I think something must have fallen on him."

Kastella said impatiently, "What's the position, Conway?"

Conway sat down. "Well, it's a bit difficult."

"What about the water?"

"Oh, they've plenty of water—thirty or forty gallons, I should think. . . . The thing is, we'll have to give them a tow."

"A *tow!* Where to?"

"To within sight of land, anyway. They're helpless."

"That's not our business," Kastella said sharply. "We've got our own troubles to worry about. Someone else will have to look after them."

"There isn't anybody else," Conway said. "There probably won't be. No one fishes out here. They've no sails and no engine. If a storm got up from the west they wouldn't have a chance. They'd blow ashore and pile up on the coral. We can't leave them."

"If we tow them in, *we* shan't have a chance, either," Kastella

129

said. "Don't worry about them, Conway—they'll get home somehow."

Conway said, slowly and contemptuously, "You bloody land-lubber!" He got up, and went back aboard the ketch.

Kastella looked at Leanda. "It's madness. . . . We just can't afford to take the risk."

"Oh, Alex," she said, "how *can* we leave them! Mike's absolutely right." She went into the saloon and rummaged among the stores and came up after a moment or two with chocolate and sweets for the children. By now there was considerable activity aboard the ketch. The young Negro was filling a small can with water from the tank. Conway was talking to the old man, gesticulating a lot and drawing painfully on his schoolboy French. The Negress was smiling happily, hugging the bandaged boy, while the little girl peeped shyly from behind her mother's skirt. Presently the two men helped Conway to lift out their water tank and lower it into *Thalia's* cockpit. Then Conway fetched one of his strong warps and made one end fast to *Thalia's* stern and threw the other end to the young Negro to make fast at the ketch's bows. Kastella looked on, scowling.

Leanda said, "What's the plan, Mike?"

"I'm going to tow them to Victoria," Conway said. "I've fixed everything with them, and they understand. We shall do the last bit in the dark and take them as close in as we dare—close enough for them to be safe, anyway. When I give the word they'll cast us off and we'll motor straight out to sea again without stopping. If the weather stays calm, everything should go smoothly. We've got all their water, apart from the gallon or two they'll need on the way, so we won't have any more worries on that score. It strikes me as a very satisfactory arrangement."

Kastella said, "You're a fool, Conway—a sentimental fool. Somebody's sure to see us. . . . You're throwing away twenty thousand pounds."

"I don't think so," Conway said, and started the engine. As *Thalia* gathered way, the ketch swung in astern of her. Conway hauled the tow line short, so there'd be no danger of it catching in the propeller, and made it fast again. Then he took his seat at the tiller. Leanda went and sat beside him. Conway looked up at the young Negro, who was squatting in the bows of the ketch, and gave the thumbs-up sign. The Negro grinned happily. Back in the ketch's cockpit, someone was singing. Kastella gave Conway an ugly look and went below.

As soon as *Thalia* was on her course, Conway started to make some calculations. It was a hundred and fifty miles to Victoria. The ketch was towing well—they should average, he reckoned, about five knots. A hundred and twenty miles in the next twenty-four hours if the flat calm held. Then a final dash in the dark . . .

Leanda suddenly cried, "*Alex,* what are you doing?"

Conway looked up sharply. Kastella was standing by the saloon door. He had the shotgun in his hand, and he was pointing it at them.

"All right," he said, "don't move, either of you." He advanced slowly. "This is where you start taking orders from me." He continued to approach until he was only a few feet away. Then, still watching Conway out of the corner of his eye, he turned the gun on the young Negro in the ketch's bows. "Let go that rope," he called. "Let it go, boy, or I'll blow your head off."

For a moment the Negro seemed paralyzed. Kastella pointed

to the rope and jerked the gun. The gesture was more effective than any words. Suddenly the boy flung himself on the rope and cast it off.

"Keep her going, Conway," Kastella said.

The ketch quickly fell away astern. The Negro boy was shouting. Soon the others joined him in the bows, crying and gesticulating. The gap widened. A long, despairing wail came over the sea. It sounded like "Na pas di leau . . ! Na pas di leau . . !"

4

The gun was pointing at Conway again. Kastella's face had the closed look of a man who'd made up his mind on a course of action and meant to go through with it. His fore-finger was crooked round one of the triggers in a very business-like way. Conway had to fight the urge to turn his head away from the barrels. A blast of shot in the face at that range! Sweat poured off him.

"Be careful, Kastella!" he said. His mouth was dry—words came with difficulty. "You'll never get to Africa if you press that thing too hard, you know."

"That's true," Kastella said. "Of course, the opposite is also true. Unless I have good hopes of getting to Africa, there'll be no particular reason why I should be careful. It looks as though co-operation is in both our interests."

For a moment there was no sound in the ship but the beat of the engine. Then Conway said, "Is it all right for me to get the tow rope in?"

"Of course."

Conway hauled the trailing rope clear of the propeller and silently coiled it. Leanda was staring at Kastella and the gun as though she were hypnotized.

"Now let us get back on our proper course," Kastella said. "To the west!"

Conway moved the tiller over and took *Thalia* round in a tight half circle until she was heading into the evening sun. As they swept past the motionless ketch, the wailing broke out again. Leanda suddenly came to life. "You can't leave them," she cried. "Oh, you *can't!*" She half rose from her seat.

"I must," Kastella said. "Sit down and keep still. . . . Full speed ahead, Conway!"

For a second, Conway hesitated. The gun jerked. Conway bent and opened the throttle wide. "You callous, double-crossing bastard!" he said softly.

Kastella shook his head. "Not callous, Conway—just realistic. Not double-crossing, either—the arrangement to tow them in was yours, not mine. I warned you not to make it."

"They've only enough water for a day or so," Conway said. "At least you could stop and give them a bit more—we can easily spare it."

"We don't *know* that. Didn't you say this passage could take weeks? I'm determined to run no more risks."

"Not long ago you were prepared to cross on five gallons!"

"That was when there seemed to be no alternative."

"It's murder, I tell you. They'll die of thirst."

"I hope not, Conway. If they do, it can't be helped."

134

"Oh, it's wicked," Leanda cried. "It's monstrous. . . . How *can* you?"

"I have to put first things first, Leanda. Our people need me. You know that. You came on this expedition because you knew it. Now success is within sight. We can't risk throwing everything away."

"But those poor people, those children . . . !"

"In time of war," Kastella said, "the innocent always suffer. Spyros is at war. The people of Spyros are suffering, too. They, too, are being murdered—by the English. This is no time to be squeamish."

Leanda gazed at him incredulously. "I scarcely recognize you," she said. "You talk like a stranger."

"It could be that you never really knew me," Kastella said, with a thin smile.

By now the ketch had fallen far behind. The cries were growing faint. Leanda looked appealingly at Conway. "Mike . . . ?"

He shrugged. "What can we do?"

She got up, white-faced, ignoring the gun. "Can I go below?" she asked.

"Certainly . . ." Kastella stepped back to make way for her, the gun still at the ready. "But I warn you not to do anything silly. You'll only get—very badly hurt."

She walked past him into the saloon and closed the door behind her.

There was a little silence after she'd gone. Conway sat

hunched over the tiller, his face wooden. Presently Kastella said, "I know what you're thinking, Conway."

"I'm thinking you've lost a supporter," Conway said.

"That's not all. . . . You're thinking how you can get this gun away from me."

"Maybe."

"I'd be surprised if you weren't! Then, when you'd got it, you could go back and find the ketch and tow it into Victoria. You're an obstinate man."

"I'm a careless one," Conway said. "I ought to have thought of the gun."

"Well, you didn't—and now it's too late. You won't get it away from me—I shall see to that. I've handled guns before, you know."

"That's pretty obvious."

"During the war, when I was in the Resistance, I learned all the tricks. . . . It's as well you should know. In any case, in a few hours it'll be impossible for you to go back to the ketch, because you wouldn't be able to find it again. Am I right?"

"I guess so."

"In a few hours, then, perhaps we shall be able to come to a sensible understanding . . . ?"

Conway said nothing. He continued to sit crouched over the tiller, his face a mask of blankness.

It was a fantastically strained night. At dusk, Kastella took up a position on the coach roof, with a supply of food and water —and the gun. From there, he could command the cockpit in safety and make sure that Conway didn't attempt to change course. Leanda prepared food for Conway and herself and did her two-hour stints at the tiller as before, but she hardly spoke a word. She had the dazed look of someone whose whole world had suddenly crumbled about her. Conway was silent, too, watching for any slip on Kastella's part. Once, just before a change-over, he thought he saw Kastella's head droop on his chest and took an experimental step away from the tiller—but the gun came up at once, and he didn't try it again. The engine beat steadily on. The flat calm persisted.

At dawn, Conway took star sights and worked out their position. They had covered ninety-six miles during the night and were more than three hundred miles from Heureuse. Leanda prepared breakfast in silence. Her eyes were red—she looked as though she had been crying.

When the meal was ready, Kastella waved her to the stern with Conway and climbed cautiously down and backed into the saloon. He breakfasted with the gun pointing out of the door. Then he returned to the coach roof. He looked a bit tired, but he was still in full command. Conway topped up the fuel and checked the supply in the spare tanks. The engine was doing well, using less than he'd expected. Leanda went listlessly through the essential jobs below. The day was already blazing hot, without a breath of wind. Waves of heat came up from the engine; waves of heat poured down through the awning that Conway had rigged again. On the coach roof, Kastella had pulled out a corner of the stowed mainsail and made himself a bit of shade.

It was Conway who broke the long, suffocating silence.

"Well," he said, "I reckon those people on the ketch will soon be down to their last pint or two if this goes on."

Leanda said, "*Don't*, Mike—I can't bear it."

"It's going to be a sizzling day," Conway said, looking at Kastella. "Those kids'll be in a bad way before long. Especially the one with the cut head. They'll soon be as dried up as their shark meat."

Kastella stirred. "There's no point in dwelling on it, Conway."

"We could still go back," Conway said. "We *might* find them. . . . How would you like to die of thirst, Kastella?"

"What's done is done," Kastella said. "It's all over."

"All over?" Conway shook his head. "I should say it's just beginning for you! When the news gets out that you deliberately left five people to die of thirst, your reputation in Spyros is going to be damaged quite a bit."

Kastella said, "Heureuse is a long way from Spyros."

"Sure—but news travels."

"If this news travels," Kastella said, "it will travel by way of the English—and in Spyros nobody ever believes what the English say. They've been trying to blacken me ever since I took over the leadership—there's never a week goes by without them thinking up some new accusation. My people never pay any attention—they know it's all propaganda. The reaction's automatic—and it will be the same this time. So you see, I'm not at all worried about the news getting out. . . . Besides, aren't you forgetting something?"

"What am I forgetting?"

"If those people survive, as they may do, it will prove they had enough water and were in no real danger, so they'll have no serious ground for complaint. If they die of thirst, no one will ever know what I did."

Conway eased up a section of floorboard with his foot and gave the grease cap on the stern tube a couple of turns. "There were witnesses," he said. "Leanda and myself. Remember?"

Kastella gave a bleak smile. "Well, I hardly think I've anything to fear from you, Conway. You, after all, are going to take me to Africa—not merely because I have a gun, but because you intend to earn your twenty thousand pounds and keep this ship that you're so fond of. And you're not likely to go spreading it around the world that you knowingly carried a callous murderer to safety for money, are you? I think I can rely on your discretion. As for Leanda—I *know* I can count on her."

"Do you?" she said.

"Of course, my dear girl. At present you're shocked and angry at the methods I've had to use; you're full of a very understandable compassion. But in the end you'll agree that I was right. You'll realize how unimportant yesterday's incident was against the general background of our struggle. Spyros comes first—and you belong to Spyros. You belong to the liberation movement, whatever your personal feelings may be at this moment. You've already served it magnificently, and you'll go on doing so. Your allegiance is to it—and to me, its leader."

"It *was*," she said. "Until yesterday, I think I'd have given my life for you. Now, things have changed. The man I believed in, and followed, wouldn't have done what you've done. I don't acknowledge you any more. I don't trust you any more. I—I think you might be an evil thing for Spyros."

Kastella said, "That's dangerous talk, Leanda."

"Dangerous?"

139

"If you translated it into action, very dangerous." He regarded her thoughtfully for a moment. "If you were to spread hostile reports about me—stories about abandoned fishing boats, for instance—you would be undermining our work and helping the English. And you know how the movement treats those who help the English, don't you? You remember the village of Meos, and what happened to Sophianopoulos and Kalides and the rest? Even worse things could happen to you. . . ." He paused again. "And no doubt *would* happen."

Leanda gazed at him in mingled horror and disbelief. "I—I don't understand. . . . You were against what happened in Meos —you denounced it. Now you sound as though you *approve*!"

Kastella's smile was sardonic. "You know," he said, "I think it's about time I told you some of the facts of revolutionary life— if only to stop you doing anything rash. . . . The truth is, I am not quite the person you imagine. I denounced what happened in Meos, yes, but I wasn't against it. On the contrary—I *ordered* it!"

She stared at him. "*You . . . ?*"

"Who else? I lead the movement—the whole movement. I *am* the movement. And it had to be done. You cannot win freedom for a country without ruthlessness."

She had turned very pale. "But you were always against terrorism. Those speeches you made . . . !"

"My dear Leanda, a good leader must be a Machiavelli. The world dislikes terror. Terror is bad publicity. So there must be a constitutional front, a respectable front. The leader must denounce violence. He must appear a humanist, and talk of rights and dignity, and urge conciliation and negotiation. In that way,

140

he wins over not merely the neutrals, but also wealthy romantics like your friend Metaxas, so that the coffers are kept filled. The real work, the fighting, must be done secretly through lieutenants, with guns and bombs. With care, the leader can thus have the best of both worlds—he can reap the fruits of moderation, *and* of terror. And that is exactly what I've done. Not that it is much of a secret now in the top ranks of the movement. You and Metaxas have been too long away from Spyros."

"When the ordinary people know," Leanda said, "they will never forgive you."

"Not if I fail, my dear. But if I succeed, I shall be doubly a hero. My deceit will be wisdom, and my severity, courage."

"Meos wasn't just severity! It was a hideous, unforgivable crime. A ghastly atrocity . . . Do you know what they *did?*"

"I know very well. Traitors and fainthearts have to be eliminated with the maximum of violence and terror and pain, so that others may profit by the lesson. In this case, the lesson was most effective."

"And you think that can lead to freedom and happiness!"

"It can lead to victory!"

There was a little silence. Kastella, looking pleased with himself, fingered his gun. Conway stared at the compass. Leanda said, after a moment, "At least I know now that I owe you no allegiance. I hate and loathe everything you stand for. . . . I came to Heureuse because I believed in you. I shall never cease to regret it."

"It's a little late for second thoughts about that, isn't it?" Kastella said. "What you should think of now is your own safety, your own future. If you talk unwisely, you will suffer, as the

141

traitors of Meos suffered. You have been warned! But if you are discreet, and forget the unpleasantnesses of our trip, there may be great possibilities for you. In a little while the English will have left our country, and I shall take over supreme power."

"Then God help Spyros!" Leanda said. She stood looking out over the sea, her eyes brimming with tears. After a moment, she went below.

Kastella said, "Well, Conway—you took no part in our little argument."

"No," Conway said.

"For an Irishman, you're remarkably silent. You consider it a family matter, perhaps?"

"Hardly!"

"Then, as a realist, you must surely agree with me."

"As a realist," Conway said, "I think it's men like you, on all sides, who are turning the world into a hell."

"I see. . . . In that case, any more discussion might be rather arid. What about the practical question—getting to Africa, and your twenty thousand pounds?"

"That's another matter. . . . We're still heading west, aren't we?"

"True—but it would be so much pleasanter if I felt I could count on your wholehearted co-operation."

"I'm thinking about it."

"Good! Well, now I shall go and get some sleep." Kastella climbed cautiously down from the coach roof. "I shall lock my cabin door, of course, just to be on the safe side—and I always wake at the slightest sound. So don't try anything foolish."

He glanced around the empty sea, looked at the compass, and gave a little nod. "Just keep her as she is!" he said.

The sun blazed down all morning, grilling the deck. The only breath of air was the warm draft made by *Thalia's* own passage. Conway, left alone in the cockpit, steered from under the awning. Every now and again he took a drink of tepid water from a jug beside him. He had to have it, though it almost choked him. The picture of the ketch was starkly vivid in his mind. The Negro family must be frying like eggs in their stationary craft. . . . He tried not to dwell on it, but the picture wouldn't fade.

Below, all was quiet. Leanda, he decided, must be sleeping. Lunchtime came, but no one made any move. Conway didn't mind—he had never felt less hungry. He didn't even mind Leanda not coming up for her watch. She was probably exhausted after that shattering talk with Kastella. Anyway, he was glad to be left alone. He had a great deal to think about, and a big decision to make. . . .

Soon after midday, a light breeze sprang up from the west, ruffling the sea. Conway hadn't expected that. Presently he switched off the engine and hoisted sail, setting *Thalia* on a course to the southwest. The breeze persisted throughout the afternoon, bringing a few merciful clouds. A little of the tenseness began to go out of his face; a little hope began to creep in. If only the wind would keep on blowing gently from the same direction!

Around four, Leanda came out. She looked strained, and very

pale. There was something almost furtive about the way she closed the saloon door behind her before joining Conway in the cockpit.

He said, "Have you had a good sleep?"

"I haven't been sleeping—I've been thinking. . . ." She sat down beside him. "Mike, I've got to talk to you."

"Go ahead," he said, "there's no charge."

"It's about Kastella. . . ." She was keeping her voice very low. "You must have thought me extraordinarily naïve, the way I behaved about him."

"Not extraordinarily."

"But I was. . . . After all, I scarcely knew him."

Conway shrugged. "You had bad luck. He might have turned out all right. Average for a politician, anyway!"

"I was crazy to be so trusting. I know that now. . . . I only hope it's not too late."

Conway glanced up at the sail and hauled in the mainsheet a little. "What do you mean by that?"

"Mike, he can't be allowed to go back to Spyros. He's wicked. He's a destroyer, a fanatic. All he wants is power for himself. If he ever gets it, he'll ruin my country."

"I wouldn't be at all surprised," Conway said. "For a time, anyway."

"Mike," she said eagerly, "we don't *have* to carry out our original plan. I know it sounds fantastic, going to all this trouble and then wanting to undo everything—but the situation's changed completely, and there is still time. We don't *have* to take him to Malindi. Couldn't we sail straight into Mombasa harbor—and hand him over to the authorities?"

"So that's what you've been thinking up!" Conway said.

She nodded. "I've been going over and over everything. . . . I've been in torment, Mike!"

He looked at her grimly. "If Kastella meant what he said, it's nothing to the torment you'd be in if you helped to hand him over. Not when he got free again. He looks to me like a man with a long memory."

"If necessary I could change my name, disappear. . . . Anyway, I'll have to take a chance."

Conway shook his head. "You won't need to. I couldn't take him to Mombasa even if I wanted to. We've already told him about Malindi—we've described it to him. A quiet, dark little beach. Mombasa's a blaze of lights from the sea. He'd know what we were up to at once, and he'd stop us. My guess is he'll keep that gun by him until he's satisfied he's been put ashore in the right place."

"That's probably his plan—but perhaps we could get the gun away from him."

"I don't think so. Haven't you noticed how he holds it all the time—with his firing finger on the trigger and his left hand low down on the barrel? It could come up in a split second. Even if he didn't fire it, I couldn't hope to get it away. In a struggle, he'd just about eat me."

"I know he's much bigger and stronger," Leanda said, "but there must be some way of dealing with him."

"Like knocking him on the head . . . ? No thank you, it's much too risky. . . . Besides, aren't you overlooking something rather important?"

"You mean the money you're going to get?"

145

"Exactly!"

"No, I hadn't forgotten that. But I think Victor Metaxas would be glad to pay you for *not* letting Kastella go, now. When he made his agreement with you he had no idea what a horrible genie he was going to let loose—any more than I had."

"You can't be certain of that. For all we know, he may be secretly behind Kastella."

"I'm sure he's not!"

"You were sure about Kastella!"

"But, Mike, remember how Kastella spoke of him."

"That's nothing to go by—if they were in cahoots Kastella might not want us to know about it. . . . In any case, I can't take a chance on Metaxas changing his mind. He may be a romantic in politics, but he must be shrewd over money or he'd never have got where he has. He promised to pay me if I delivered the man to an agreed spot. That's morally binding on him. If I make entirely new and contrary arrangements, to suit myself or you, I can't expect payment and I don't believe I'd get it. No man is going to pay out twenty thousand pounds on a broken contract."

Leanda said, "You'd still have the boat, Mike."

"I wouldn't even have that—not legally. In spite of all the funny business with Ionides, it's not in my name."

"Well, I don't see what Victor could do about it."

"He could do plenty if he wanted to. . . . Anyway, I wouldn't care to keep the proceeds of a contract I'd broken. What I want is the twenty thousand, fair and square."

"But Mike . . . !" Leanda broke off, in deep distress. "Oh, I know it's a terrific lot of money, and I've absolutely no right to

146

ask you to abandon it—but then you *were* ready to risk it all over the ketch, weren't you? You were going to tow the boat in, even though you said yourself there was a fifty-fifty chance of our being caught."

"That was different," Conway said. "There were lives at stake. Now there aren't."

"There'll be lives at stake on Spyros. You've seen what Kastella's like; you know what he's capable of. . . . Mike, you once told me that your way of life, sailing around the world in a boat, at least didn't do any harm to others. You rather prided yourself on that. But if you help Kastella now, if you use your skill for that, you *will* be doing harm. Terrible harm."

"I'll be doing what I contracted to do," Conway said. "What *you* helped to persuade me to do. . . . Look, Leanda, you know perfectly well that I only undertook this trip because of the money. I made that plain right at the beginning. It was a paid job. Kastella meant nothing to me, nothing at all. He was your hero, not mine. *You* were starry-eyed about him, I wasn't. I don't like him any more than you do—but then I never did, right from the first moment I set eyes on him. But that didn't stop me carrying on. Why should I stop now?"

"Surely it makes some difference—the way he's behaved? You said yourself he was a murderer. You were as angry yesterday as any man I've ever seen. You looked as though you'd throw him to the sharks if you could. I don't understand you. Have you forgotten so soon? Does it really mean so little to you?"

"As far as the ketch is concerned," Conway said, "I could have been wrong about him being a murderer. I'm keeping my fingers crossed."

147

"What do you mean?"

"The wind's been heading us all afternoon. If it's blowing the same where the ketch is, the boat must be moving steadily in toward the shore. The east-going current's carrying it along, too. If the wind holds for a bit longer, they'll be taken over the banks and some other fishing boat should see them before their water gives out. I'd say they've a fair chance of surviving after all."

"Oh, *Mike* . . ." Leanda's face was suddenly bright with relief. Then it clouded again. "You're not just *saying* this?"

"To justify myself for going on . . . ?" He pointed to the close-hauled sail. "You can see for yourself."

"Oh, I do hope you're right. . . . I haven't been able to get them out of my mind for a moment." She looked again at the sail, as though reassuring herself. Then she said, "All the same, it doesn't change a thing about Kastella, does it? *He* didn't know there'd be a wind from the west. He's still a murderer at heart."

"That's quite true. But it does make it a little easier for me to finish my job and take my money."

"And what about Spyros?"

"Spyros means nothing to me. It never has. It's not my business to try and set the world to rights."

Leanda looked at him, and shook her head. "You've changed so much, Mike—do you know that? On the way out, you'd have said that with a sort of smile, not quite meaning what you were saying, knowing you weren't really as indifferent as you were pretending to be and that anyway your conscience was clear. . . . Now you say it savagely, and I know perfectly well why. So do you."

"Maybe," Conway said.

148

"Mike, you say Spyros means nothing to you. . . . I suppose I don't mean anything to you, either?"

He gave a little shrug, scowling down at the floor. "I like you, Leanda—you know that. We got on pretty well together on the way out—and on Heureuse. You're—well, you're a nice kid. I'd have liked things to turn out the way you wanted them, for your sake. But I'm certainly not prepared to make tremendous sacrifices for you. Why should I? If I did what you're asking, and tried to get that gun away from Kastella, I'd probably finish up with half my face blown off and I'd certainly finish up without a bean —or a boat. If I do what's good for me, I'll have twenty thousand pounds *and* a boat." He hauled in the sheet a little. "We're going to Malindi."

Leanda said, in a low voice, "Is that your last word?"

"It is."

"Well, I can tell you this—*I* shan't help you to get to Malindi. You can count me right out. In fact, I'll do everything I can to prevent you."

"That's up to you," Conway said. "I dare say Kastella and I can manage."

"You'll actually work with him!"

"Why not? We're on the same side. Both out for ourselves!"

"I think you're utterly contemptible!"

"Perhaps. At least I'm frank."

Leanda jumped up, her eyes blazing. She looked around the cockpit. Suddenly, without any warning, she snatched up the seven-pound lead from its place under the coaming and brought it crashing down with all her strength on the compass at Conway's feet. Before he could make any move, the damage was

149

done. The glass top was crushed in and the delicate instrument destroyed.

"*Now* see if you can find Malindi!" she cried.

Kastella came out of the saloon so quickly that Conway decided he must have been listening behind the door. "What's going on?" he demanded. He swung the gun round at hip level, his eyes narrowed against the bright sunlight.

"I'm afraid Leanda's a bit overwrought," Conway said. "She got angry with me and started smashing things."

"What things?"

"Now don't fly off the handle, Kastella—the damage isn't irretrievable. It's the compass, actually. . . . Pity!—it was a lovely job."

Kastella said, "The *compass!*" He stepped across and had a look at the shattered face. Then he swung round menacingly on Leanda.

"Easy!" Conway called. "I tell you there's no real harm done— I've got a hand-bearing compass that'll serve perfectly well. It'll be a bit awkward, but we'll manage. . . ." He shook his head sadly. "Leanda, that was *very* stupid."

Leanda looked from one to the other. "You make a fine pair!" she said. "A murderer and a mercenary, and not a human feeling between you. God, how I loathe you both!"

She turned, and rushed below.

Kastella said, with satisfaction, "So you've decided to be sensible, Conway?"

"I've decided I can't afford to pass up twenty thousand

pounds, if that's what you mean."

"That's exactly what I mean. I'm only surprised it took you so long to make up your mind."

"I might not have made it up now," Conway said, "if things hadn't changed quite a bit. . . . It looks as though that ketch will make the land after all—this wind is blowing it toward the shore."

"I told you you were exaggerating the danger."

"I wasn't—it's just a bit of luck. Don't misunderstand me, Kastella. I'm not playing along with you for the sake of your beautiful eyes—I think you're just about the foulest thing in human shape that I've ever come across. When I put you ashore at Malindi, it'll be to save my skin and get my money—and that's all."

"I quite understand," Kastella said. "You've already made it plain that you're hardly an admirer of mine!"

"There's another thing—you'll have to turn to and do a lot more work. Leanda hates my guts now as much as she hates yours, which is saying something! She won't help me, and even if she would I couldn't rely on her any more. That means you'll have to take watches and sail the boat for part of the time."

"I'm in your hands, Conway. Naturally I'll do everything I can."

"Very well . . ." Conway frowned. "How do you feel about being out here on your own at night? Do you think you could handle her in the dark?"

Kastella looked at him warily. "In the dark?" He fingered the barrel of the gun. "No, I think perhaps you'd better take charge at night."

151

"In that case, you'll have to sail her all through the day, or I shan't get my sleep. It probably is the best way—you shouldn't get into much trouble in daylight. Of course, if the weather turns bad I'll relieve you at once. All right?"

"Perfectly."

Conway eyed the gun. "Do you still plan to carry that blunderbuss about with you all the time?"

Kastella smiled. "If you don't mind, Conway, I think I will. Not that I don't trust you—our interests are obviously identical. But it does provide an additional assurance—just in case for any reason you should change your mind. And, of course, there's always Leanda's temperament to consider."

Conway shrugged. "Have it your own way," he said. "But watch your trigger finger, that's all. Leanda's probably going to be a damned nuisance to both of us, but she's a fine girl and she's in my care. If anything happened to her, I'd throw in my hand regardless of consequences. Is that clear? There's going to be no bloodshed, even accidentally. You can keep that stuff for your private torture chambers."

"You put things so nicely, Conway."

"I put things plain. You said I was a realist, and so I am. . . . Right now you'd better take over while the sailing's straightforward. . . ." He stood away from the tiller so that Kastella could move in. Then he opened up one of the side lockers and brought out the hand-bearing compass and some tools. In a few minutes he had improvised a bracket for it.

"You'll find this thing swings a bit more than the other one did," he said, "but it'll be accurate enough for our needs. The course is 220. Anyway, all you can do at the moment is keep her as near the wind as she'll sail."

Kastella nodded. "Where are we, roughly?"

Conway glanced at the patent log. "By this evening," he said, "we should be just coming up to the halfway mark. Five hundred miles to go."

5

From now on, Conway realized, life aboard *Thalia* was going to be dominated as much by Leanda's hostility as by Kastella's gun. She had already shown what she was capable of, and she might well be plotting more acts of sabotage. The first thing he did on leaving the tiller was to move all his charts and navigation tables, his sextant and chronometer and radio, to the lockers in the cockpit, where they would be constantly under the eye of Kastella or himself. Kastella nodded approvingly. Then he made some sandwiches and a flask of coffee to take out with him for his night watch. It would be easier, he decided, if both he and Kastella looked after their own requirements from now on. Leanda was evidently going to do nothing for them. Lying on her bunk, she seemed completely indifferent to everything that was going on. When Conway offered her coffee, she said "No thank you!" with frigid politeness. It was going to be, he thought, one hell of a trip! Presently he went into Kastella's cabin and lay down there. The two ports were opaque with crusted salt and he could see neither water nor sky, but he could tell by *Thalia's* slight heel and steady motion that Kastella was doing all right.

As dusk fell, he went out into the cockpit to take over once more. The transfer, this time, was awkward. Kastella seemed reluctant to leave the tiller untended, but when Conway stepped forward to take it he jerked the gun and ordered him sharply to keep his distance. He was much more on edge, now that the light was failing, and Conway hadn't much doubt why he'd decided against doing any night shifts. Their alliance was obviously going to be a very uneasy one. Conway told him quietly that the ship would be perfectly safe if he let everything go. Kastella moved back then, and as *Thalia* came up into the wind Conway took the tiller and sheet and soon brought her back on course. Kastella peered down into the lighted saloon and went cautiously below. Through the open door, Conway heard him telling Leanda to go into the forecabin while he prepared food for himself. He was clearly going to take no chances. Conway wondered how he'd manage these tricky maneuvers when the weather got bad. It would be a lot more difficult for him, then.

The evening passed quietly. Kastella didn't come out into the cockpit again, and around ten Conway heard him carefully locking the door of his cabin. Leanda moved around for a while in the saloon, and then she, too, went to bed. Conway settled down to his long night watch. It was peaceful and pleasant in the cockpit after all the excitement, and once more he felt glad to be alone. From time to time he ate a sandwich and drank some coffee. Occasionally a flying fish hit the sail and fell on the deck with a light plop. Nothing else happened. The wind continued to blow gently from the west all through the night. Con-

155

way watched for the first glow of dawn. As the sun came up astern of *Thalia,* Kastella appeared on deck, the gun crooked under his arm. He looked very cheerful. He glanced at the log, and gave a satisfied nod. They had clocked nearly forty miles during the night.

The wind was still westerly, but light and safe. Conway, tired and aching after his twelve-hour shift, turned in immediately after breakfast, leaving Kastella in charge. Leanda, stubbornly neglecting all the chores, went up to her old place in the bows. For her, Kastella might not have existed. Kastella struggled along at the tiller as best he could, but the morning was nothing like as fruitful as the night had been. By noon, when Conway emerged, they had logged only twelve miles through the water, and some of that had been lost through drift and leeway.

"You're pinching her too much," Conway said, watching Kastella's efforts. "You're trying to sail too near the wind."

"I'm trying to keep on course," Kastella said.

"I know, but it doesn't help in the end—you only lose way. Try and keep her sails full."

Conway stayed for a while, supervising. Then he went below, and got some food, and did the neglected routine jobs. Afterward he spent a busy hour or two boiling up linseed oil and putting a dressing on the galvanized steel wire of the standing rigging.

At dusk he took star sights. It was Kastella, now, and not Leanda, who held the stop watch while he used the sextant. When the sights were taken he started to explain the principle by which the position of the ship was calculated but Kastella cut him short and said it was time they changed over. He was obviously much less interested in the calculations than in the little penciled crosses that were once again creeping across the track chart. Conway could see him, back in the safety of the saloon, studying the chart carefully. It showed that in the past twenty-four hours they had made good forty-nine miles.

Soon after dusk the wind started to die away. Conway sat on for a while, using the sails as long as he could. He was steering now by the light of a hurricane lamp, since the dial of the hand-bearing compass was not illuminated. Leanda was in the cock-pit, too. Kastella had sent her out while he prepared the evening meal. Her face looked impassive in the glow of the lamp. Con-way wished he knew what she was thinking, what she was plan-ning. She was altogether too quiet for comfort. Once or twice he tried to jolly her into talk, but he had no success.

Slowly the old doldrum calm settled over the sea again. Pres-ently Conway went forward and lowered the sagging sails. "I'm going to use the motor, Kastella," he called down. "There's no wind." Kastella shouted an acknowledgment. Conway started the engine and returned to the tiller. He glanced at the patent log and opened the throttle. Leanda retreated to the coach roof, away from the engine noise. A quarter of an hour passed. Con-way looked at the log again. Suddenly he frowned. He picked up the hurricane lamp and held it close, so that he could ex-amine the log line. It seemed to be rotating quite normally. He continued to watch the dial for a moment. Then he cut the en-gine.

"Kastella!" he called.

The cabin door opened and Kastella stuck his head out warily.

The lamp light gleamed on the gun barrel. "Something wrong?" he asked.

"Was the patent log working properly when you left the tiller?"

"As far as I know, yes."

"Well, it isn't now—the indicator isn't moving. . . ." Conway glanced sharply up at the coach roof. "Have you been fooling with it, Leanda?"

"No, I haven't," she said. "How could I; when you were there all the time?"

"I wasn't here when I was taking the sails down."

"Well, I didn't touch it."

Kastella advanced a step, and stopped. He looked as though he thought the whole thing might be a trick to get him out into the dark. "What are you going to do, Conway?"

"Find out what the trouble is, if I can. I expect I can fix it." He wound in the log line, got his tools from the locker under his feet, and unshipped the instrument. "I'll have to take it inside," he said. "I'll need more light."

"All right," Kastella said. "But just move slowly, will you!" He stepped to the side of the cockpit and Conway went below with the log and the tools. Kastella watched him through the door, trying to keep one eye on Leanda at the same time. For a while, Conway busied himself with a screwdriver. Then there came a sound of hammering.

Kastella said, "Have you found out what's wrong?"

"Yes, one of the small cogs has sheared. I'm trying to burr the spindle, but I don't think it's going to work. Like to look?"

Kastella hesitated. "I'll take your word for it," he said.

158

There was more hammering. Presently Conway came out with the log in his hand. "No, it's no good," he said. "I'll have to try and solder it in the morning."

Kastella said, "How important is it?"

"The log? Well, it's essential for dead reckoning, of course, but in these latitudes we ought to be able to rely on pretty regular sights, so we'll probably manage whatever happens. It's a nuisance, though."

"Could Leanda have done it?"

Conway thoughtfully regarded the silent figure on the coach roof. "If she'd suddenly heaved hard on the line, that might have done it. Or the cog could just have sheared itself. I guess she's entitled to the benefit of the doubt—this time!"

Leanda said nothing.

Conway put the log carefully away in the cockpit locker and started the engine again. Kastella went below and finished his supper. Presently Leanda went in, too.

Conway ran *Thalia* all night under engine, with the throttle well open. Now that he had no log he could only guess at the ship's progress, but in a dead flat sea he reckoned she must be doing a good eight knots. The morning sights confirmed it. The little cross that he put on the track chart was more than a hundred miles further to the west.

"That means we've about three hundred and fifty miles to go," he told Kastella, as he handed over. "And I must say I'll be damned glad when we get there." He sounded very tired. This second unbroken watch of twelve hours, with the engine pounding away at his feet all the time, seemed to have drained him.

159

Kastella looked around the empty sea. Directly astern of them, the sun was shooting up in a hot ball, threatening another blazing day. There was no hint of wind.

"It's a pity we haven't enough fuel to motor all the way," Kastella said.

"Well, we haven't. . . ." Conway ran his hand over his eyes in a weary gesture. "All right, Kastella—keep the sun behind you and you won't go far wrong. I'm going to get some sleep."

He went below. Leanda was lying on her bunk, her face turned away. She didn't stir. For a moment he sat looking at her, thinking nostalgically of the companionable trip they'd had on the way out. Then he stretched out on the berth and tried to compose himself. The engine beat sounded in his ears like a sledge hammer. He got up and closed the door and tried again. Without air, the heat was stifling. After about five minutes he gave it up and went out into the cockpit.

"You'll have to switch that damn thing off for a bit, Kastella," he called irritably. "I'll never get to sleep."

"Why don't you go into my cabin?" Kastella said. "The engine didn't worry me there."

"It'll worry me. Engines always do—I hate the bloody things. Give it a rest—we can only use the fuel once." He waited while Kastella switched off. "If the wind gets up, call me, and I'll come and make sail for you. If it doesn't, for God's sake let me sleep. I'm just about all in."

He went back into the saloon and lay down again. *Thalia* was rocking gently on the quiet sea. In a few moments he was asleep.

It was well on in the afternoon when he reappeared—washed,

160

shaved and wearing a clean shirt. The long rest seemed to have transformed his spirits. He nodded briskly to Kastella and took a quick look round. A breeze was beginning to get up, still from the west, and there were a few clouds about. "Right," he said, "shall we get cracking?"

"It's about time," Kastella said surlily. "I was just going to call you." He was sitting hunched in the cockpit with the gun on his lap.

"Oh, come, you mustn't grudge the maestro his sleep!" Conway said. "After all, we want to keep this a happy ship, don't we?" He climbed to the coach roof and prepared to hoist sail. Leanda was up in the bows. "Hullo, Leanda!" he called.

"Hullo!" she said in a flat voice.

He grinned. "It's good to be alive—you ought to try it sometime." He hauled the mainsail up and swigged the luff taut. Kastella took the tiller, and in a few moments they were under way, on the same southwesterly course as before.

Presently Conway got out the patent log and the soldering outfit and went into the saloon to try and fix the sheared cog. It was a fiddling job, and it took him over an hour. Even then he wasn't very satisfied with it. "Let's give it a try, anyway," he said. Kastella moved away from the helm while he fitted it and streamed the line. In about ten minutes there was a perceptible movement in the figure on the clock face. For an hour, the log worked normally. Then Kastella reported that it had stopped again.

Conway shrugged. "To hell with it, then! We'll do without it."

There was too much cloud for sight taking at dusk. In any case, Conway said, it would hardly have been worth the effort,

161

since their position had changed so little during the day. The transfer at six was made without incident. Kastella, following what had now become his regular routine, got food for himself in the saloon and then went immediately into the forecabin and shut himself up there. Leanda left the deck, and Conway settled down to another long night watch.

The wind blew steadily from the west until just before dawn. Then it backed to the southeast. Conway looked thoughtful. Presently he hove to and went to have a look at the barometer. It had gone down a little. After a moment he took the small sea anchor and a warp from one of the cockpit lockers and carried them up onto the foredeck, where he was occupied for some minutes. There was nothing like being prepared for all eventualities!

The clouds dispersed around ten, without giving any rain. The breeze continued to blow gently from the southeast, keeping the sails nicely filled. With a fair wind, it was possible at last to steer *Thalia* due west. Conditions could scarcely have been better— but Kastella, doing his first spell at the tiller with the wind aft, was having considerable difficulty.

"She won't keep on a straight course," he complained, as he struggled to get the ship under control again after his fourth jibe. "First the head swings to the left, then it swings to the right."

"Well of course it does if you let it," Conway said.

"I can't stop it."

"That's because you're not used to running. . . . You've got to keep a firm grip on the tiller all the time and correct each

162

movement before it happens. Look, let me show you. . . ." He stepped forward. Kastella snatched up the gun and covered him.

"Sorry!" Conway said. "I forgot you were still nervous." He waited while Kastella moved out of the way. Then he got *Thalia* back on course and held her steady. The muscles of his forearms stood out in knots as he gripped the tiller. "See?—she's perfectly all right. You'll get the knack of it in time. . . ." He handed over again. "Anyway, I don't think you'll come to much harm. Do the best you can—I'm going forward to take a nap."

He went below and collected his straw hat. Then he climbed up into the bows and seated himself with his back to the mast, looking down at the water. *Thalia's* bow wave was scarcely more than a ripple—they certainly weren't moving very fast toward Africa and twenty thousand pounds. Still, they were moving. The sun, streaming down over his left shoulder, was hot. He pulled his straw hat over his neck and leaned back, smiling. Things weren't going too badly. After a while, he dozed off.

The wind remained in the southeast for the next twenty-four hours, blowing just hard enough for good sailing. Conway had his most satisfying night shift for some time. Kastella, on the other hand, continued to complain of difficulty with the tiller and seemed to be no nearer mastering it. By the end of his watch he looked quite exhausted. Progress during the twenty-four hours had been only fair. Conway put their position, at the end of the fourth day, some two hundred and sixty miles east of Mombasa.

That evening the breeze died away and the sea took on a pale

sheen like mother-of-pearl. Kastella, increasingly restive, urged
Conway to use the engine again, and once more they had a noisy
night motoring through a flat calm. By morning the crosses on
the track chart had taken another hundred-mile leap.

The calm persisted, and after Conway had had a short sleep
he let Kastella use the engine too. Then the water pump began
to give trouble. Conway, still tired after the night and in a very
bad temper, spent most of the day on his knees in the fierce heat,
dismantling and cleaning the pump and fitting a new washer,
while Kastella looked on and chafed and Leanda sat silent and
unhelpful in the bows. By the late afternoon, when the job was
done, Conway swore he had lost half a stone in sweat. But the
engine was working perfectly again, and as there was still no
wind Conway ran it all through another night, though at half-
throttle to conserve the much depleted fuel store. What was left,
he said, they would have to keep now for their final dash to the
coast—wind or no wind.

In fact they had a measure of luck. A light breeze returned
during the morning—but once again it was heading them, so
that their progress was not very good. Kastella sat all day at
the tiller, as *Thalia* slowly beat to the west. He was showing in-
creasing signs of physical tiredness with every trick at the helm
—but Conway had only to make a sudden movement to dis-
cover that his watchfulness was as great as ever.

That evening, the sixth since their meeting with the ketch,
the glass fell sharply and the head wind strengthened. The sea
got up quickly, and *Thalia* began to pitch in a way she hadn't
done since the big storm. Kastella cut short his evening meal,

took some Dramamine, and locked himself away in his cabin to get through the unpromising night as best he could. Leanda, untroubled so far by the lively motion, stayed on deck. She seemed less aloof than usual, and even held the boom steady for Conway while he tucked a precautionary reef in the sail.

"What's this—a change of heart?" he asked, as he rejoined her.

"No, Mike—but there's something I must say to you."

"If it's something nice I'll be delighted to hear it. I've missed our friendly chats."

"It's about Kastella again. . . ."

"Then I'd say you were wasting your time."

"Do you still feel the same about trying to get the gun away from him?"

"Exactly the same."

"I'm sure we *could* get it, Mike, if we worked out a plan together. I've been thinking. . . ."

"I'm sorry, Leanda—there's absolutely nothing doing."

She was silent for a while. Then she said, "Mike, has it occurred to you that Kastella might have plans for *us?*"

"What do you mean?"

"Well, we know all these frightful things about him—what he did at Meos, and the ketch, and so on. It's only guesswork, after all, that the people on the ketch got back safely. He may actually be a murderer. He's tried to terrorize me into keeping quiet, and he pretends he can rely on your discretion—but he must be quite worried."

"He could be."

"And he's utterly ruthless. He's also got a gun. Mike, how

165

do you know he won't kill us before he leaves the ship, to make sure we keep quiet?"

"I *don't* know."

"Have you thought of it?"

"Indeed I have."

"Then how can you *not* do anything about the gun?"

"Because," Conway said, "I think the risk that he'll try to kill us is much less than the risk of trying to get the gun. . . . It's a gamble I've decided to take, and I think it's a fair one. Anyway, I've put altogether too much into this business to give up when we're hardly more than a hundred miles from land. It's no good, Leanda—I've made up my mind and I'm going through with it." He hauled in the mainsheet and braced his foot against the locker as *Thalia* heeled. "It looks as though we should have a pretty good sail tonight!" he said.

The wind blew hard for several hours, but its strength never approached that of the first storm. *Thalia* took quite a tossing, but there was no menace in the seas and Conway thoroughly enjoyed his spell at the helm. By four in the morning he was able to shake out the reef and carry on under all plain sail. He was just eating the last of his sandwiches when he was startled by a loud crash below, and the sound of shouting voices.

At once he let the sheet and tiller go and dived for the saloon. Leanda wasn't in her bunk. Kastella's door was half open. Through the gap Conway caught a glimpse of figures struggling wildly round the barrel of the gun. He hurled himself forward. There was a shattering report as the gun went off. The door slammed in his face. He put his shoulder to it and went stagger-

ing into the cabin as it flew open. The gun barrel jabbed hard
into his stomach. "Don't move!" Kastella said.

He looked wildly round. Leanda was lying face downward
on the floor, moaning. Ignoring the gun, he dropped to his knees
beside her. "*Leanda!*" he cried. "Oh, *God!*" He turned her over,
dreading what he might see. But there was no blood. He could
see no injury at all. Her eyes flickered. "Leanda," he said, "darling—are you hurt?"

"She's not hurt." Kastella was crouching back on his bunk,
pointing the gun down at Conway. "Not much, anyway. I had
to hit her. She'll be all right in a minute."

"You swine!" Conway said.

"It was better than shooting her, wasn't it? I'd warned her
what to expect. She's lucky."

"Why didn't you lock the door, you damned fool?"

"I did lock it. She must have loosened the screws while we
were on deck—look, you can see. She tried to snatch the gun
before I was properly awake. It went off accidentally." He
pointed to the shattered white wood of the cabin roof that could
so easily have been Leanda's face. "Then I hit her."

There was a sudden lurch as *Thalia* came broadside onto a sea.
Left to itself, the ship was being tossed about like flotsam. Kastella's greenish pallor grew more sickly. "Get her out of here,"
he said.

Conway lifted Leanda and carried her tenderly into the saloon. She stirred as he laid her on her bunk. He fetched cold
water and dashed a little of it into her face. She came round
quickly. In a few moments she was fully conscious again. Except

167

for a bruise at the side of her chin, she seemed none the worse
for what had happened.

Conway sat over her, shaking his head. "You silly, crazy kid!"

She lay still, looking at him. "I had to try," she said. "I had to
do something. . . . *You* wouldn't."

"Of course I wouldn't. I didn't want to. I told you it was too
risky. . . . God, it's a miracle you're not dead."

"I almost wish I were," she said.

None of them referred to the incident afterward. Leanda,
more shaken than she'd realized, stayed in the saloon all day, but
made no fuss. Conway looked after her as well as he could, avoid-
ing any further reproaches. The only effect on Kastella was to
make him still more cautious. He had cleaned and reloaded the
gun, rather ostentatiously. Conway could scarcely make a move
now without having it trained on him.

The sea grew steadily calmer during the morning. By eleven,
the westerly wind was light. Kastella was at the tiller. Conway,
six feet away from him, was studying the chart of the African
coast. The last penciled cross on the track chart, made after
dawn sights, had put them only eighty miles from Malindi.

As he laid the chart down, Kastella said, "Well—what do you
think?"

Conway glanced up at the close-hauled sail. "If we keep her
as she is, we should be about sixty miles from Malindi by dusk.
The fuel's low, but there should be enough for that distance.
The barometer's steady, the weather is going to be all right. I
think we should be able to make it tonight."

"Splendid! What's the timetable, then?"

"Well, if we start the run-in, say, at seven, we should be through the reef and anchored in the lagoon off Ionides' place between four and five in the morning, with a bit to spare. There'll be no one about at that hour, so you'll have no trouble, and it'll still allow time for me to get clear with *Thalia* before daybreak. It's vital I shouldn't be seen off the coast, or they may put two and two together and start looking for you."

"I agree. . . ." Kastella looked at him thoughtfully. "And what are your own plans, after that?"

"I think I shall make for Portuguese East—it's as good a bet as any. I should be able to refuel there—and maybe get a cable through to Metaxas."

Kastella grinned. " 'Mission accomplished please send twenty thousand pounds'?"

"Something like that."

"It should help to make you a welcome visitor."

"It'll make *me* feel a lot better, once I've got my hands on it, I can tell you that. And I reckon I've earned every penny of it. I wouldn't say this trip's been exactly easy."

"No . . . You'll be taking Leanda with you, of course."

"I'll have to. If I put her ashore with you, she'd give you away at once. *And* I wouldn't blame her."

Kastella ignored that. "She's going to be a bit of a problem, Conway, all the same. What happens while you're rowing me in? She could sound the hooter, show lights, get up the anchor—anything."

"I know," Conway said. "I thought of that. I'll take the lamps out of the forecabin and lock her in. She won't be able to

169

do any harm there."

"What about the broken door?"

"I'll fix the screws—it's quite a simple job." Conway picked up the chart again and began to draw a sketch on the back. "Now here's the layout for you when you get ashore—it's very straightforward. Sandy track, parallel to the lagoon, among the coconuts. The first building you'll come to will be Ionides' shack, a white one. We'll probably see it from the dinghy, anyway. You know where to find the key. I've marked the telephone box. I don't think you can go wrong. Here, have a look. . . ." He got up suddenly and moved toward Kastella.

The gun jerked. Kastella's finger was tight on the trigger. Sweat stood out on his forehead. "Careful!"

Conway threw the chart down on the seat and stepped back with a grin. "Gosh, you're jumpy!"

"I'm not taking any risks."

"You still don't trust me?"

"To be frank, not entirely. . . . I happened to overhear part of a conversation you had with Leanda, early on in this trip. She was urging you to take me into Mombasa and give me up."

"If you heard that," Conway said, "you must have heard my reply. I said it was impossible, because you had the gun, and that anyway I didn't want to."

"Quite so—and your answer was very reassuring. . . . But you could still change your mind."

"And lose my pay after all the trouble I've gone to? Why on earth would I do that?"

"Because you're fond of Leanda."

"I'm quite fond of her, certainly, but . . ."

"You're *very* fond of her, Conway. I've got eyes and ears. When she and I had our little difference over the gun, you called her 'darling.' "

Conway smiled. "That was just force of habit. Don't forget we were playing man and wife for quite a while."

"It didn't *sound* like force of habit," Kastella said. "It sounded quite heartfelt. It was all the more impressive because when you called her 'darling' she was unconscious! I've had to ask myself whether your affection for her might not be stronger than your desire for money."

"Well, the answer's no. She's not my type—not in that way, I've no taste for political bluestockings!"

"She's got a very nice leg inside the stocking."

"I dare say, but the answer's still no. I'm fond of her, but I'm much fonder of twenty thousand pounds. You'll see."

"Oh, I believe you," Kastella said. "I just like to be cautious, that's all. Hence the gun!"

Conway gave a little nod. "Talking of caution," he said, "I don't entirely trust you, either. Maybe this is the time to raise the matter."

Kastella regarded him impassively. "Well?"

"I'm not saying this is likely, but Leanda and I do know a great deal about you—all of it highly unpleasant—and it seemed just possible you might try and silence us before you went ashore."

"The idea never crossed my mind."

"I find that hard to believe," Conway said. "But I certainly advise against it—in your own interests. If you shot Leanda, you'd naturally have to shoot me. You could get rid of our bodies easily enough, but you couldn't get rid of *Thalia*. She'd be found

171

at once. Long before you could get out of Kenya, there'd be an inquiry and a search. Ionides would refuse to help you, and you'd be caught."

"Very probably," Kastella said.

"Almost certainly. . . . Of course, you may be thinking you could scuttle the ship, and that in that case she *wouldn't* be found. . . . But that's just the point. If you scuttled her outside the reef and tried to row yourself in through the swell, the dinghy would be swamped and you'd be drowned. And you couldn't scuttle her inside, because the water in the lagoon is only about six feet deep, and she'd show. . . . I thought I'd mention it. I should hate to be shot because of a technical miscalculation!"

"I understand," Kastella said. "Happily, the problem doesn't arise. As I told you, I'm not in the least afraid that *you* will talk. I shall warn Leanda again before I leave, though I can't believe it's necessary. In any case, I very much doubt if she could do me serious harm. . . . So you'll find, Conway, that *your* suspicions are misplaced, too."

The day drew to a close with a clear sky and almost no wind. Conway took special care over his dusk sights and got a perfect fix from three stars. The penciled cross put *Thalia* sixty-three miles due east of Malindi. They were all set now for the last dash to the coast. Both the men had an early evening meal, since the ship would have to be darkened for the run-in and it would be difficult to move about. Kastella prepared himself for the shore, and Conway removed the lamps from the forecabin and explained to Leanda why she would have to be locked in there

172

later. She protested that it was unnecessary, that she had no more plans for making trouble, but when she found that Conway was adamant she retired there voluntarily, saying she was going to bed. After her effort of the night before, she seemed to have lost all hope. Conway doused the lights in the saloon, while Kastella waited outside. Then he rigged a piece of sailcloth as a shield round the hurricane lamp in the cockpit and started the engine. Kastella returned to the dark saloon and lay down on one of the bunks with the gun barrel pointing toward the tiller.

It was a tense passage for both men. Despite their mutual assurances, suspicion charged the air. Kastella, it was clear, still feared he might suddenly find himself at the entrance to a lighted port. Conway still felt uneasy about what Kastella might do when they arrived off the coast. In addition, he had the considerable sea hazards to worry about. This was by far the most difficult part of the whole trip. Unless he could make a perfect landfall, all his earlier efforts would have been wasted. He watched the compass constantly.

No sound came from the forecabin as they pounded steadily through the night. Once, around two o'clock, Kastella stuck his head out and looked about him, but there was nothing to be seen except empty sea. Conway, wholly preoccupied with navigating the ship, replied curtly to his few questions, and he soon withdrew again.

At four, Conway suddenly throttled the engine down to half speed. Kastella was out of the door at once. "What's happening?"

"I can hear the reef," Conway said. He let the engine idle for a moment or two while Kastella listened. From somewhere not

173

far ahead of them came the menacing roar of surf. They must be very near the coast now, but there was still nothing to be seen. Apart from a few stars, there wasn't a light anywhere.

"No wonder they call it the Dark Continent!" Conway said.

Kastella gazed anxiously toward the surf. "Will you be able to find your way in?"

"I'll tell you that later!"

"Are you sure it's the right spot?"

"I'm not *sure*, no—I just hope it is! Anyway, it's not Mombasa, is it?"

"It's not Mombasa," Kastella agreed.

"I told you I wanted my money," Conway said.

They were going dead slow now. The air was very still. Scents from the land hung over the ship. The surface of the sea was calm, but there was a troublesome swell. Suddenly Conway said, "Look!" and pointed. Kastella, gazing ahead, saw a line of white foam on the water. The noise of the surf was much louder. Conway turned *Thalia* parallel with the reef, so that her bows faced northward. This was the most anxious time of all. He had deliberately aimed for a spot well south of the gap, so that by turning north he'd be sure of finding it. He had navigated with all the skill and care he could command—yet he might easily be several miles out. He looked at his watch in the dim light of the hurricane lamp. Nearly half past four! They were cutting it pretty fine. He stood on the seat by the tiller, peering ahead. Five minutes passed. Ten minutes. The gap should be visible by now—they must have covered more than a mile along the reef. . . . Suddenly, a satisfied "Ah!" escaped him. There was

174

a break in the line of foam on the port bow. It was only a short one, and at close quarters he decided he didn't much like the look of it—if he got into a blind pass, a cul-de-sac, in the dark, he'd be in real trouble. . . . He kept going. Soon there was a new break, a wider one. He closed in cautiously, watching the surface of the water for any fleck of white. He was no longer thinking about what Kastella might do when they arrived. If they hit the coral, the problem wouldn't arise! Slowly the yacht nosed forward. . . . Yes, this looked more like it! To port there was no surf at all now—only a surging mass of black water. Conway put the tiller hard over and turned into the gap. The ship started to swing broadside on in the swell, rocking violently, and he had to open the throttle wide to keep control. For good or ill, they were committed now. *Thalia* raced ahead. Gradually the noise of the surf receded. They were in the lagoon! Conway took a wide sweep round behind the reef. Soon the rocking ceased, the water grew calm. They were safe. He switched the engine off and let the ship glide on silently till she lost all way. Then he went forward and quietly lowered the anchor over the bows.

"Well, we've made it!" he said softly, as he rejoined Kastella in the cockpit. "And though I say it myself; it was a bloody good bit of navigation." He pointed shoreward, with a sailor's pride in a good landfall. Against the starry sky, coconut palms were silhouetted in a pattern that he recognized. From their depths came a faint gleam of white. "Ionides' shack," he said. He bent to turn out the hurricane lamp.

As he straightened up again, Kastella's gun poked sharply

175

into his ribs. Conway was suddenly very still.

Kastella gave him a slap on the back. "I just wanted to congratulate you," he said. "Well done, Conway!"

They wasted no time. Quickly but silently, Conway launched the dinghy. Kastella went forward to make sure the forecabin door was locked. "Good-by, Leanda!" he called. "Don't forget what I said—about talking. I meant it, you know!" There was no reply. After a moment he left her. Conway had the dinghy at the stern. Kastella climbed in, still clutching the gun. The dinghy dipped alarmingly under his weight. Kastella pointed the gun at Conway. "No last-minute tricks!" he said. "I don't want to have to swim for it!" Conway picked up the oars and began to row in, very cautiously, aiming for a spot a hundred yards or so beyond the white gleam.

The shore was close. A tiny breaking wave marked the edge. In a few moments the dinghy's forefoot scraped lightly on the sand.

Kastella got out. He stood for a second looking down at Conway. "Well, I suppose I can't expect you to wish me luck!" he murmured.

"You're dead right. I reckon I've done a pretty lousy thing bringing you here. All I hope now is that they catch you and jail you for life!" Conway started to shove the dinghy out.

"Wait!" Kastella broke the gun, emptying the cartridges out on the sand. "You can take this now. . . . You may need it to protect yourself from Leanda!"

Conway silently took the gun, and pushed the dinghy off.

176

FOR LEANDA

He rowed quickly, till he could no longer see the dark figure on the beach. Then he relaxed. It was all over—finished! Suddenly he began to laugh. Once he'd begun laughing, he couldn't stop. He was so convulsed that he could scarcely row. He tried to stifle the sound, but his whole body shook with the gigantic effort to control himself. He was still laughing as he tied the dinghy to *Thalia's* stern. He gave a great shout of laughter as he opened Leanda's door. Inside, he rolled against her bunk, doubled up with mirth.

She said, in an icy tone, "Have you gone mad?"

"*I've done it!*" he said. "I've done it! Oh, *God!*"

"You've done a terrible thing. . . . I'll never forgive you."

"There's nothing to forgive," he said, rocking helplessly. "Absolutely nothing to forgive."

"What do you mean?"

"You won't be hearing any more of Kastella for a long long time. I've just put him ashore on Heureuse!"

6

Leanda said, "Now tell me how you did it!"

It was an hour later. They had cleared the island on the last of the fuel and the engine had just sputtered to a stop. Conway had hoisted sail, and *Thalia* was ghosting westward in a light air with Leanda at the tiller. The sky had a look of dawn about it, but they were far enough away now for safety. The sense of urgency had gone with the engine beat. At last they could talk.

Conway said, "It was simpler than you'd think."

"It couldn't possibly have been simple."

"Well, there was a lot in my favor. Kastella knew nothing about navigation, don't forget, and hardly anything about sailing. . . ."

"Start at the beginning," Leanda said. "When did you first think of it?"

"Oh, when Kastella was sitting up there on the coach roof, threatening you with nameless horrors. I knew I'd got to do something—I'd made up my mind about that after the ketch incident. But I knew there was almost no chance I could get the

178

gun away from him, and without the gun I couldn't do anything against his will. Then, as he was talking, I happened to notice that we were coming up to the halfway line and that old phrase 'the point of no return' came into my mind and I suddenly wondered if it need be and if I couldn't take him back to Heureuse and kid him it was Malindi. The coastlines were similar, and both had reefs and lagoons—they even both had a white building near the beach. . . . Anyway, that was the start of it."

"Couldn't you have told me, Mike? It would have made such a difference. . . ."

"I know, but it might have made the wrong sort of difference. It was absolutely vital to the whole plan that you should make Kastella believe you and I were on opposite sides, so that—up to a point—he'd trust me, and you did it beautifully when you called me all sorts of names and smashed the compass. Your attitude had the ring of truth about it because it *was* true, and it stayed true all through. Kastella had his moments of doubt, but basically he was pretty sure I meant to earn that money. If you'd known of the plan you'd have had to act your part, and he might easily have seen through it."

"Yes, I see," Leanda said. "I suppose you're right—though it was one of the most ghastly weeks I've ever spent. . . . Anyway, go on."

"Well, you both played into my hands beautifully. *You* refused to help with the ship, which left Kastella and me to split the work between us. He still had a sneaking fear I might try to get the gun, so he let me do all the night watches and kept well out of the way after dark. That was perfect. All I had to do was

179

wait till you'd both retired and then turn the ship round. That first night, when I was supposed to be beating to windward, I actually ran nearly sixty miles the other way. The ports in Kastella's cabin were so salted up he couldn't see the stars, so there was no danger there. Of course, if he'd had the slightest feeling for a ship he'd have known we weren't beating, but fortunately he hadn't."

"I didn't realize it, either," Leanda said.

"You're still quite a novice, too. Besides, all *you* could think of was how to get the gun and how much you hated us both. As far as the running of the ship was concerned, you were practically sleepwalking."

"That's true."

"Anyhow, no one noticed anything, and that first night went off splendidly. Just before dawn I turned the ship round again. Then Kastella took over and sailed her all day, but he was so new to it that we only made a few miles—so that was all right. All the same, I could see a pretty big snag looming up . . ."

"The log!" Leanda said.

"Exactly! That was one thing he was *very* interested in—the number of miles we were covering. I realized he'd be bound to get suspicious if he found me regularly clocking up fifty miles or more on what was supposed to be a hard night's beat, when the best he could do was ten miles in a day—and anyway, there was another difficulty. Each time I took sights, I had to tell him we were roughly as many miles west of center as in fact we were east of it, so that when I finally made a landfall in Heureuse he'd be all ready for it in Africa. I saw it was going to be quite impossible to square the phony positions with the actual log eadings. So I had to get rid of the log!"

"What did you do to it?"

Conway grinned. "As a matter of fact, I didn't do anything to
it to start with. I said it wasn't working and took it off to mend
it. When I got it into the saloon I hit it with a hammer. Kastella
was so scared about coming close, he couldn't see what I was
doing. Next day I botched the soldering job, and the thing came
unstuck, and that was that."

"And he probably thought I was responsible all the time!"

"Probably—you were most useful as a whipping girl. . . .
Well, that was the major headache disposed of, and I motored a
hundred miles to the east that night without giving anything
away. But using the engine raised another problem—Kastella
naturally wanted to use it too. I let him, for a short time—remember?—and then I threw a fit of temper and said I couldn't
sleep. So he pretty well wasted his day shift."

"Mike—it must have been terrifically exciting."

"It was a bit of a tightrope act—I wasn't at all sure it was going to work out. But things went pretty well. I had another good
night, running east when I should have been beating to the west.
Then, just before I handed over to Kastella, I sabotaged what
should have been a good day's run for him."

"How . . .? I don't remember anything."

"Don't you remember he kept complaining about the steering?"

"Oh—yes."

"Well, he certainly had reason to! I'd streamed the small sea
anchor from the bows on a very short rope. It's weighted, of
course, so it went down under the ship, holding her back and

181

spoiling the steering. Kastella had a fair wind and the sails were full and he should have been eating up the miles, but actually he was getting nowhere fast—especially with the east-going current against him all the time. It makes me blush now to think of the tripe I talked about the difficulties of steering before the wind!"

"But, Mike, suppose he'd discovered! The top of the rope must have been visible from the foredeck."

"Of course, but he never had the chance to see it. I streamed the thing in the dark each time, before he took over at the tiller. Then I went and sat beside it for most of the day, ready to cast off if he came up to the foredeck. But he didn't—he had his job to do and he stayed in the cockpit. And you didn't, either, because you were giving me the cold shoulder. In the evening, when you were both safely below, I hauled the sea anchor in for the night. It *was* a bit of a risk, of course, but it came off. . . . After that the wind dropped, and I had to organize the spot of bother over the water pump."

"You mean that was sabotage, too!"

"Indeed it was. I put a bit of cloth in the filter just before I handed over. I knew Kastella would want to go on using the engine, as it was a flat calm, and I didn't want to *seem* to stop him a second time. But I had to, somehow—we were only about a hundred and sixty miles from Heureuse by then, and if he'd done a hundred miles to the west it would have ruined everything. So I put the engine out of action and spent all day fooling with it."

"I'd never have guessed. You seemed to be working terribly hard."

"I was—I took a lot of things to pieces that I didn't need to . . .! Anyway, that was about the end of my worries—except for the final dash. There was a tricky problem of timing, there—if we went in too close during daylight, Kastella would see the outlying islands and know we were in the wrong place. If we didn't get close enough, we wouldn't reach Heureuse before dawn. Actually, we were just about right. I had some anxious moments getting through the islands with that compass, and I was terrified I wouldn't be able to find the gap in the reef again. . . . But we made it!"

"And my only contribution," Leanda said in a tone of disgust, "was practically to get myself killed."

"Since you didn't succeed, I'm prepared to admit now that it was a jolly fine effort. It helped to maintain the right atmosphere."

"Well," Leanda said after a moment, "it all seems too incredibly wonderful to be true. To me, at any rate . . . What about you, Mike? Do you still think you won't get the money?"

"I think Metaxas would be pretty crazy to pay. But perhaps he'll let me keep *Thalia*. I hope so."

"I hope so, too. . . . It'll still have been an awfully big sacrifice."

Conway grinned. "I reckon I've had value for it."

"How?"

"I've settled my score with Kastella—and it was a pretty long one. First he tried to push me around. Then there was the ketch. Then there was the way he threatened you. Quite simply, I hated his guts. Losing the money was a small price to pay for the pleasure of putting him back on Heureuse right under the bungalow we took him from. In fact, it was a self-indulgence!"

"Oh, Mike!"

"Anyway, it's been worth it, just to have you looking at me as though I'm a human being again."

"Does that matter so much?"

"Indeed it does."

Leanda said, "You know, I don't think you'll ever make much of a living as a mercenary!"

The ship glided slowly on through the cays. The sky grew lighter. The sun rose in a magnificent array of color. Everything looked incredibly peaceful. Leanda, gazing around, gave a deep, contented sigh.

"It's like the journey out," she said. "Just the two of us again—and everything so lovely and quiet." She smiled. " 'The great out-of-doors . . .' "

Conway nodded. For a moment he was silent. Then he said, "Oddly enough, I remember the end of that quotation now."

"Quotation? Oh, the one about living out of doors?"

"That's right."

"Well—tell me."

Conway said, " 'To live out of doors with the woman a man loves is of all lives the most complete and free.' "

Leanda looked up at him. Tears suddenly glistened in her eyes. "Well, darling, we're going to have at least a thousand miles of it, aren't we?"

"At least!" he said.